# Alexander
# And the Academy of
# Good & Evil

*A H Daniels*

# Dedication

I dedicate this book to my dear, loving wife, who has endured with me through its entirety.

# Acknowledgment

To start, I thank the Almighty God for granting me an extensive imagination and blessing me with Godly people who raised and supported me. To Mom and Dad, thank you for teaching me invaluable lessons to help me grow and understand God's teachings. To my Wife Laura, I'm exceedingly grateful for you and your input in my life helping me to grow and become a better man of God. To my siblings, cousins, and teachers, I thank you for all the bits of wisdom and knowledge you have imparted to me over the years. And finally, I would like to thank my publisher, Jaydon, for he and his team, who have worked extremely hard to make this book refined and beautiful. May this book bless the lives of many, and to God be the glory.

# Table of Contents

# Prologue

In an era long past, within a realm where expansive waterways stretched wide and profound, vast marshlands teeming with viscous reptilians and expanses of wheat and corn fields sprawled across the dominion, bestowing sustenance and refuge to creatures both large and small.

Perched regally at the juncture of aqueducts, amidst a stern procession of fir trees along the embankments, stood a manor of slate-blue grandeur. Its tri-level spire towered over the neighboring buildings, encompassing a harmonious workshop and a diminutive sunroom. A shutter clattered against the mansion's side as gusts howled and lashed. Beneath the somber, pendulous clouds, a narrative of mystery and madness is set in motion.

The duo of silhouettes approaches the abode. They hastened along the winding concrete walkway, bypassing the colossal alabaster columns, towards the large timber door. The dame promptly taps upon the ajar entrance before gliding to console the inhabitants.

A gentleman unlatches the wooden door, permitting entrance. He swiftly surveys the desolate footpaths and carriageway for onlookers. Perceiving none, he seals the substantial door and fastens it securely.

Facing the matron, he exclaimed, "Please hurry; she's up the stairs," his voice urgently laden.

The matron darts past the elongated banquet fixtures and surges up the winding staircase, her medical satchel thudding against the railing as she gradually advances toward her patient.

Mr Complicated, the household patriarch, greets the gentleman accompanying the lady. In silence, they proceed to the parlor, where the lighting is subdued, and Mr. Complicated's five children slumber deeply on armchairs, divans, and one strewn across the floor. The blaze in the masonry fireplace radiated intensely, casting capering silhouettes upon the luminous ochre walls and ceiling, soothing the spirit and kindling the heart of Mr Complicated. He musters a brave smile, understanding of the imminent trials and the destiny he is to confront in the swiftly nearing future, for which he had long braced himself.

He tenderly surveys his quintet of progeny, to whom he and his consort have imparted the Light Arts of the Master. His name resounds, prompting him to ascend the stairwell with all speed, his companion in close pursuit. They navigate stealthily to the upper sanctum, a place destined for irrevocable transformation.

Navigating the shadowed corridor, they arrive at the bedroom door and veer left. He fortifies himself before breaching the threshold while his associate lingers without. Within, Mrs. Complicated and the matron are seated, cradling an infant newly ushered into the world.

Mrs Complicated beams and outstretches her embrace; he advances, enfolding her in his arms. The governess tenderly transfers the diminutive baby into their custody before departing, the door whispering shut in her wake.

"Could he be the prophesied one?" Lucil queries, her gaze laden with melancholy. "I don't know; he awaits outside to tell us." Yet the babe was naught but an infant. "How shall he know for certain?" "I know not, my love, yet we shall invite his scrutiny upon the youth when you deem it timely." Their eyes collectively ponder the babe. "Should he be the chosen, the Soul Snatcher shall covet him fiercely," Lucil muses.

"It is for this cause we must endow him and consign him to an esteemed academy, there to forge formidable alliances," Bartimus contemplates, his eyes a reservoir of affection and resolve.

"Admit the seer," she consents. A venerable figure, his visage shrouded by a hoary beard, enters. With fervor, he advances, claiming the child. His examination is meticulous; lifting his gaze to the anxious parents, he imparts his whispering verdict.

"Choose me!" "No, I am the chosen!" Two lads stand defiant, their eyes ablaze, fists clenched, visages aflame with anger. "What good do you possess? You swine of the refuse realm!" "Pardon, you vermin of the highlands!" "Hold it; give me a moment to think!" Alexander Complicated interjects amidst his companions. One is a recent acquaintance, hailing from his soon to be new home; the other is a lifelong confidant. Presently, he contemplates his crossroads.

Should he select a comrade for his impending cross-country move or...? The Soul Snatcher's specter looms. His mother's teachings of impartiality beckon him to obey them. Would he require the companionship of Ben (a name shared by both peers)? Upon his departure... The sinister persuasion within whispers, coaxing him to declare, "You, Ben!" His gaze settles on the newcomer.

Ben, the childhood ally, retreats to his abode atop the adjacent elevation, his spirit shattered. Glancing back, he observes Alexander and the other Ben navigating the path home, threading through the shorn fields and woodland.

Yet, Alexander's soul is in disarray, and his heart is defiant of tranquillity.

Amidst the fog, a cloaked entity grins, his teeth yellow with age. His red eyes betray naught but conquest. In sotto voce, he vows, "My Child, you shall yet be mine."

********************************

"But Mom, please. I don't wanna go!" Alexander moans to his mother.

It was the first day of fall, and he and his siblings were to start learning at the Academy of Good and Evil. There, they would learn Mathematics, Geometry, and, first and foremost, The Arts of the Master.

His mother attempted to reason with him, "You'll come home on vacation, and I'll visit you as well; school doesn't last forever. Besides, your friend Lucy will be there on her first day too."

"But why can't I go to school with Ben?"

"Because he and his family are Non-Light Followers".

"But can't he be like me?" Alexander questioned further.

"Yes, he can if he chooses to when he's older." His mother assured him. "But now is not the time to wonder and question. Just do as you're told."

Just then, the Academy Bus sounded its horn outside. The children grabbed their bags, and with their mothers' encouragements ringing in their ears, they boarded the 72-foot four-decker white school bus that would take them far from home for a time.

(To clarify to the reader, when they grab their bags, it much more resembled their rooms, for they each had one large tote for clothes and shoes, two regular bags for books and writing tools, and one briefcase for everything else a child could need for a school term.)

Of course, the bus boys and drivers loaded all these bags underneath the massive bus. Oh yes, there were six drivers on this bus. The bus had six sets of tires: two in the front, two in the middle, and two in the back.

It was a tricky business where each driver was responsible for a tire, so when they came to a corner, they would all have time to turn their wheels in unison to complete the turn.

Besides six wheels, it also had 240 windows and 4 levels. Each level was equipped with 17,576 seats. Each level was assigned to specific age groups. The first level begins with ages 12 and 13, the second for ages 14 and 15, the third for 16 and 17, and the fourth and final level for ages 18 through 21. Oh yes, a magnificent bus it was, with an elevator to go up and down and lavatories at the back. It also included a kitchen that would trolley through bringing delightful snacks and candies, making one's mouth water at the thought and sight of them.

A small girl with little blonde hair and sky-blue eyes sat at one window. She wore a simple flower dress and little white shoes. Suddenly, she bolted upright, tugging on her friend Tarah beside her.

"Look!" She exclaimed, "It is Alexander, my friend, the one I told you about!"

Tarah glanced over, annoyed, as Lucy's excited yelling interrupted her examination of her new coloring book. She was a slip of a girl with brown eyes and goldish hair. Her parents were royalty in the LF (Light Followers), so her clothes resembled those of an overdressed Barbie, with ruffles, designs, and so much extra posh it would make one's eyes roll.

"Alas, what a gaunt, diminutive, unsightly youth!" Tarah declared with a disdainful air.

"Truly, observe him! Sable locks, brown eyes, bland clothes— such an abhorrent boy! Would you not concur, Charlotte?" She solicited the opinion of her companion.

"Indeed, and the cap? Should he tug it further down, he'll smash into obstacles," Sarah retorted.

"Only then would he merit attention." The pair exchanged mirthful glances while Lucy gazed forlornly through the pane as Alexander entrusted his luggage to the attendants. She continued her vigil as he progressed towards the conveyance's ingress.

"Wow! Such towering doors," Alexander mused. The vehicular doors spanned from the ground to the fourth tier, with railings ensuring the safety of any overzealous show-offs.

"Make haste, young sir! We have numerous halts ahead," the driver interjected, jolting Alexander from his reverie.

Regaining composure, he inquired, "Pardon, sir, but to which seat am I assigned?"

"Your name, lad?" probed the driver.

"Alexander Charles Complicated, Sir," he responded meekly.

"Very well, Alexander Charles Complicated. Behold three seats per column, nine in total. Now, transpose the initial of your name to numerals. Thus, for you, '133', as 'A' equates to '1' and 'C' to '3'. Your designated place is the first column, third row, and third seat. Proceed forthwith; our departure is imminent."

Alexander faced the other students, their countenances marred by frowns. A cacophony of laughter and sundry remarks permeated the atmosphere.

"Didn't his parents teach him the basics?"

"I knew my seat on my first time!" exclaimed a seasoned attendee.

"Fortunate for me is my initial 'M', sparing me his proximity," another voiced.

Alexander's gaze met that of the last commentator—a robust lad with blonde, spiky hair poking out from his round head, blue eyes, and red cheeks. Though merely a year his senior, the boy loomed over him, peering down with those verdant eyes.

"A member of the Complicated lineage, I perceive—yuck, contemptible filth," he uttered. "Were it my father's decision, your kind would be barred from both the academy and colosseum! Indeed, your sort is unworthy to lick our boots."

"Be seated!" thundered the public address system. "All must be seated; we are commencing our journey," the voice reiterated.

As tranquillity descended and the pupils located their seats, Alexander's eyes met the scornful gaze of the ruddy-cheeked youth. He averted his gaze swiftly and nestled into his assigned place.

"Oh dear," he murmured.

# Chapter 1
# Beck's Bold Encounter

Alexander reclined against the window; his cranium pressed to the glass. The passing landscape blurred before his eyes. Adjacent seats remained unoccupied. Most fellow students conversed with friends or kin or had already forged new connections with their peers. In this frigid, unforgiving world, Alexander felt profoundly alone.

He sighed. His considerably older siblings occupied the upper floors. Lucy, his sole familiar companion, sat at the rear—Lucy Bee Meek, to be precise.

As the bus halted once more to admit additional students, Alexander brooded.

"Hello," a small yet assured voice chimed.

Alexander blinked; before him stood a scruffy lad with disheveled blond locks, a pugnacious nose, and slate-grey eyes. His grin revealed an expanse of teeth.

"What's your name?" he inquired, regarding Alexander with admiration.

"I'm Alexander," Alexander stammered.

"Cool. I'm Achan Beck Comrade, though everyone calls me Beck."

"Pleased to meet you, Beck. Is this your first time as well?" Alexander ventured.

Beck beamed. "Yep, but my sisters have regaled me with tales. They reside on the third floor; fear eludes me," he boasted.

Alexander feigned confidence. "Well, I'm—"

"Look!" Beck interrupted, pointing eagerly out the window.

Before them stood the imposing Academy edifice, ensconced amidst verdant lawns and shrubbery. Flowerbeds and swings adorned the nearby willow trees. As the bus approached, a gravel-lined circular drive materialized, its central fountain spouting water in a heart-shaped cascade. The Academy itself, constructed from robust crimson bricks, spanned 100 feet in width and 200 feet in length and plunged 66 stories into the earth. Twenty-seven stories soared skyward, each tier boasting varying window counts—some twenty, others fifteen, a few with seven, and some solitary. The underground levels harbored tantalizing mysteries.

Seven colossal candlestick-shaped pillars flanked the massive hickory door, supporting the white marble overhanging roof. A prominent crucifix adorned the wooden portal.

As the bus traversed the substantial stone bridge spanning the murky moat, it hissed to a halt.

The Academy's door creaked open.

"Odin's beard! That's Head Principal Carethemost!" Beck exclaimed directly into Alexander's ear. "See him?"

Alexander followed his new friend's pointing finger, alighting upon a gentleman with a profusion of red curls. Clean-shaven, with lengthy sideburns, the man's hazel eyes swept over the crowd of students disembarking from the bus. Their excited chatter overlapped. His attire—modest buttoned shirt, securely tucked into azure breeches, a cream-hued sweater enveloping most of his torso, and grey shoes— bespoke fastidiousness. As he began to speak, straight white teeth hinted at his cleanliness obsession. "Attention, pupils," he addressed the assembled group, flanking adults acknowledged with a sweep of his hands. "Welcome to the Academy of Good and Evil, affectionately known as AGE. We trust you will relish your tenure here. Before you commence your studies, allow me to introduce the four primary room instructors. For ages twelve and thirteen, I present Mrs. Good."

A short, stout woman stepped forward, her impassive countenance punctuated by a curtsey. Her black gown brushed the floor before she resumed her place in line.

"Jingle bells! What a dour hag," Beck muttered, not nearly quietly enough.

"Quiet, Beck," Alexander interjected. "You'll land us in trouble.

"But come on, look at her nose!" Beck persisted.

"She will teach you," Carethemost continued, "In the Light Arts of the Master, including some arts that you should avoid, but most importantly, she will teach the Arts you may need to apply in the future. Listen well, for she is a wonderful teacher."

"Now," he continued, "I present to you, Mrs. Joy, for the age of 14."

A young, frizzy-haired woman steps forward, her laughing blue eyes mirroring her enormous smile. She waved gently to the students, who, in their turn, excitedly waved back. She silently bounced back to her place in line beside Principle Carethemost. Her head barely reached the same height as his waist, for she was very short.

"Mrs. Joy shall help you expand your horizons in cultural differences and what is acceptable for boys and girls your age."

"For ages 16-17, Mr Shy." Head Principle Carethemost motioned to his left to a nervous-looking white-haired man with bountiful cheeks and bursting shirt buttons. He wore a waistcoat of green plaid, matching dress pants, and green dress shoes. Dipping his head, he retreated quickly.

"Lastly, the 18-year-old students in their last term. You shall be under my direct tutorship. Now Mr. Shy and I shall overlap each other in our teaching of Light Arts; we shall all work to instill Leadership principles, Purity of heart and mind, and dedication to the Master."

## Beck's Bold Encounter

"For now, we happily welcome you. Come! Explore the Academy and the grounds; your books and bags will be distributed to you in your selective cubicles. One thing to remember is that when you hear the bell, everyone is to return to the grand hall quickly and quietly.

I suggest that those of you, who do not know their placement either ask an older student or find it yourself, then explore the rest of the grounds at your leisure. Thank you!"

With that said, the teachers turned and vanished inside, all except Mrs Joy, who continued watching as the students began their exploration of this big new realm.

"Let's go, Alexander! I know where the Grand Hall is," Beck said, pulling on Alexander's shirt sleeve.

"O really, how, though?" Alexander asks as he is dragged at a steady pace up the eleven stone steps leading to the main doors, which Mr Carethemost had left open.

"How? My sisters told me, of course", replied Beck.

The hallway they entered was painted white, with timelines stretching fifty feet long. On the floor, 30 squares of 12-inch-wide marble spanned its width, and a twelve-foot ceiling with soft glowing lights illuminated the hall. In the distance, it teed off and made a left—and right-hand turn. A big sign hung on the wall at the end of the hall reading, "Boys Left-Girls Right."

"Wow, you see that?" Alexander pointed at a sign on the same wall that read, 'Boys and Girls under the age of 15 will be in bed before the clock strikes 9'.

"I wonder who wrote that, probably that scary-looking Mrs. Good; what a nose, I tell you..."

"Hush Beck! There she is".

Mrs Good rounded the corner from the girl's side. She tossed a glance at them and then continued stomping toward the main door.

"Sugar babes, the building even shakes when she walks," chortled Beck quietly.

"C'mon, where to now?" motioned Alexander. They walked left and then made a right into another hallway. The boys' Lavatories were directly on the right. Beck led on to a set of whitewashed double doors.

"And here we are!" He said, gently pushing the one door open just enough for them to stick their heads through.

Their mouths dropped open at the sight. The Grand Room was 100 ft. square, twelve massive windows adorned each wall, and two roll-up doors on either end could disappear into a magnificent 50 ft. ceiling. A massive chandelier in the center lit a perfectly round one-hundred-and-fifty-person table. The table was decorated with candles and little pieces of décor to make the female gender smile, touch it in delight, and show it to their friends. 149 red plush chairs surrounded the table. Only one chair was different. Trimmed in purple silk with a high back, the Letters HM were engraved in gold. Its huge armrests resembled that of two shepherds' staffs. A painting of thirteen men at a long table laden with food and wine stretched before them. Hung on the back wall of the Grand Hall. The Words 'Final Feast' were printed in red underneath the twenty-five-foot painting.

"See that chair, Xander?" Beck Jammed Alexander's ribs with an Elbow.

"I see it," Alexander growled, rubbing his hand on his smarting ribs. What does HM Stand for?"

"Uh, Hello, are y'all going to just stand there gawking all day."

The boys spun around, letting the door slam shut. Tarah and Lucy stood there; Tarah stood with one better-than-thou hand on her better than through the hip.

"Who are you?" spat Beck.

"Someone who is way more important than you," Tarah retorted.

"Ha, what a gargoyle-looking girl you are," Beck fuelled her anger further.

Alexander grabbed Beck's shoulder and said, "Hey, hang on, this is my friend Lucy; Lucy, this is Beck; he sat beside me on the bus."

"Hi Xander, this is Tarah, my friend from Ouster Heim. Umm, Hi Beck, nice to meet you."

Beck gritted his teeth and clenched his jaw. "Hi", He mumbled. Tarah pretended not to notice the introductions.

"So, did you get all your paper and quills?" Xander asked Lucy.

"Yes, I hope I have enough. We don't have a lot of marks to spend, but Mama said I should have enough." (For you to see, marks were the currency for which one could buy or sell.) "Don't worry, Lucy. If nothing else, I can share with you, and so will Beck."

"Me?!" Beck started violently and slugged Xander's shoulder.

"Yes, you and Tarah can too. We will all share", Xander firmly stated. "We have to look out for each other."

Tarah stuck her nose in the air, "Well, I, for one, won't be sharing with you boys, but Lucy can use my stuff."

"Now look here," Lucy started

"Yeah, look here Miss Snooty," Xander and Beck both engaged.

RINGGGGGGGGGGGGGGGGGGGGGGGG!!!!!!!!!!

"The bell, come on, let's go in." Lucy, Tarah, Beck, and Xander quickly ran inside.

# Chapter 2
# The Banquet

The pupils processed into the majestic Grand Hall, the seasoned ones setting the precedent. Children arrayed themselves along the wall while the teachers assumed their positions, flanking the grand seat occupied by Headmaster Carethemost. A hush pervaded, so profound that the drop of a pin upon the ancient flagstones could have been heard. Xander's gaze alighted upon a cerulean tapestry serving as the underlay for the banquet furnishings.

"Pray, convene, young scholars. Let the youngest among you come closest to us, your mentors, then fill in until every seat is claimed," beckoned Principal Carethemost.

A flurry ensued as the youth vied for proximity to their friends. The clamor of furniture and the chime of crockery animated the Grand Hall anew. Once settled, Headmaster Carethemost outstretched his arms across the table to invoke a benediction.

"What happens now?" Xander murmured.

"Hush! He renders gratitude to the Master," Tarah hissed, "Silence and observe."

Perplexed, Xander and Beck scanned for this 'Master,' their gazes eventually meeting the reverently bowed heads of their seniors. With a collective shrug, they mimicked the gesture. Post-prayer, the assembly descended upon the feast with voracity. A cornucopia of viands—turkey, maize, legumes, ham, sweet potatoes, beef, fowl, and bread—ensconced them. They gorged like famished wolves until they were nearing bursting.

Mr. Carethemost rose, proclaiming, "I hope you've satisfied your appetites. Now, we shall segregate you by dormitory. A dozen dorms await five for the lads, five for the lasses, and two sanctuaries for the teachers, which are off-limits save for explicit permission. Your dormitory mates shall be your comrades in study and sport and the helpers in the Light Arts." He gestured to Mrs. Good, "Kindly circulate the pouch to the student closest to you in their first term."Mrs. Good offered a sable velvet pouch to Olivia, a girl with fiery curls and verdant eyes, who apprehensively accepted it as though it held precious perils.

"Thank you, Mrs Good. Within the pouch reside five different coloured straws. Avoid the temptation to peer; select one and present it," Carethemost instructed with a smile.

The pouch journeyed to Tarah, who extracted a green straw, eliciting cheers.

As the pouch meandered amongst the children, Carethemost added, "Only you, initiates, require a straw. Returning students will retain their prior quarters. The last student to pull a straw, do me the favour of returning the pouch."

"Xander, you're the finale! You'll encounter the Head Principal up close," Beck whispered, tinged with jealousy.

Xander glanced rightward. A friendly-looking boy confirmed, "Indeed, you're the last one. I'm a second-year student now."

Beck delved into the pouch, unveiling a verdant straw with a wary squint but then beamed. The applause dwindled as Xander drew forth the final straw… also GREEN! Mutual grins between Beck and Xander ceased as they noted Tarah and Lucy, both brandishing green straws.

"Confound it to consort with them!" Beck blustered. Xander merely smiled, unperturbed.

"The pouch, Alexander," Mrs Good demanded. Xander, puzzled by her knowledge of his name, seized the pouch and hastened forward. Before the mighty seat, he handed the pouch to Head Principal Carethemost.

Carethemost took the bag, "Thank you, Alexander. I see you are to go to the Earth dorm, very well. It is an excellent Dormitory; I expect you will quite enjoy yourself." He then addressed the Assembly of students, "The five colors are red, yellow, blue, grey, and green, representing the five elements: Fire, air, water, space, and earth. Each dorm will have a selective symbol on the door, but if you still cannot find your way, place your straw in your right hand. Alexander", Headmaster Carethemost looked down at him, "Please demonstrate."

Xander unfolded his hand, allowing the straw to be free. Suddenly, it perked up and started to spin, eventually stopping and pointing off to his right. He glanced at Carethemost. "It points to my dorm, doesn't it? Sir?" he asked.

Carethemost smiled, "Quite right, you are, lad! So now, quiet everyone! Quiet please!" His voice echoed a bit louder the second time, for the hubbub of the new students had steadily grown as the older ones who already knew about the straws had moved on to games and other topics younger people fill their time and minds with.

"We will all see you in the morning. Older ones, please lead on. You all have big glory days ahead. Goodnight, everyone!" So, Mr Carethemost was excited, with many excited children gazing after him with great admiration.

# Chapter 3
# The Beginning

The older children lead the way to the different dorms. The greens, reds, and yellows exited from the door on the west while the greys, blues, and teachers took to the left. Once outside, students walked on a covered stone path leading to a roundabout where Four buildings stood tall in a line. The Green-selected student then proceeded between two buildings where the earth dormitories rested.

"Okay Julie, take the girls," commanded Henry, the lead boy who was now in his last term at AGE. He was a tall boy with wavy brown locks and a shapeless mouth and nose. He was very clean and proper. The little boys looked up to him, and the girls adored him from afar.

Upon entering the room, Xander observed that the bedrooms were categorized into four distinct sectors, each designated for an age group. The older boys ventured further into the building to locate their designated sector. Xander and Beck were led to their assigned bunk bed within the first enclosed sector and took a seat. Two other boys who had been in the previous term claimed the beds they had used before.

"Whew! I am so glad I did not get a grey straw. I noticed that the mean boy from the bus had one. Who is he anyway?" Xander remarked.

"You mean Marstin. That's his name. Marstin Foremost Jr." The black-weaseled face roommate replied.

"I'm Jonathan Humble. This is Drew Dependent." He pointed to his friend. A shy-looking boy with straight brown hair, red cheeks, and friendly-looking eyes greeted them.

"Nice to meet you. I'm Beck, and this is Alexander." Beck pointed towards Xander.

## The Beginning

Jonathan nodded, "Pleasure is ours, but don't mess with Marstin. He allows the dark works to flow freely and uses them well. We've been through a term with him already. He is a bad cracker, which you have already noticed."

"Thanks, I'll remember that," Xander said thoughtfully.

Just then, Henry walked through the hallway that connected the four rooms and opened the door to their sector. "Alright, lights out, lads," he said. "Classes are first thing in the morning, so you need to be alert and awake. Your teacher is tough, so you better pay attention. Sleep well." He then blew out the candles and turned off the lamps. "Oh, and her nose!" whined Beck.

"For Pete's sake shut up Beck." Xander moaned.

*****************************

"Attention, please!" Mr. Carethemost clapped his hands to gather the students in the entry hall. They were waiting for their introductions and first-day instructions. Chairs were arranged facing away from the great door, and a wooden podium was set up at the head of the hall. The headmaster stood behind the podium to address the students.

"Yes, thank you," Mr. Carethemost said, gaining everyone's attention. "As new students, I'd like to go over some rules. At our academy, we believe children should be themselves, but we have a zero-tolerance policy for the practice of dark works. Anyone caught practicing it will be punished. Otherwise, all floors, called Books, are accessible to everyone. Respect is crucial when dealing with AGE's property. Now, please follow your teachers to your designated rooms. Students aged 12-16, please follow me." Mr. Carethemost turned and waited as the students separated themselves according to the given instructions.

Xander and Beck shuffled to their classroom after Mrs. Good.

"What dark works do you suppose he meant?" quivered Xander.

Beck glanced over at him, "Probably terrible ones like lying and stuff." The boys came around the corner and into the classroom.

"Well, well, if it isn't the bottom feeders," a sneering, whiny voice jeered at them as they came face to face with Marstin Foremost Jr. 's glowering face. I bet your parents barely have a mark to their names. I heard they practice the art of stupidity."

"You take that back," Beck growled, clenching his fists into a tight ball.

Xander grabbed him on the shoulder, "Chill, Beck, just ignore the little weasel." A voice scoffed behind them.

"Ugh! All boys do is squabble." Tarah rolled her eyes and huffed past them on her way to her desk. Lucy passively followed behind, taking her place in the adjoining seat.

Mrs. Good walked heavily to the front of the class. "Everyone! Find your seats quickly. Once you have found appropriate seats, you may turn your spellers to page 1 and begin reading aloud together." She looked at Xander and Beck, "Boys, sit! And no whispering".

As the class hum rose to an even pitch, they blotted out the sound of footsteps as they quietly passed the rooms and vanished into an upstairs book room.

Xander questioned his teacher as they gathered around her at the classroom table on one side of the room, "Mrs Good, why do we follow the Master?" Mrs Good looked at him incredulously.

"My word, don't you know anything?" Tarah blurted out.

Mrs. Good glared at her and spoke, her voice sounding like a cold starting engine. "Strap your seatbelts."

Xander and Beck looked at their chairs. Little seat belts hung to the side. They grabbed them, and a metal clink assured them they were secure. "Now hang on," Mrs. Good said.

# The Beginning

Suddenly, the floor gave way, and their bodies pulled at their seatbelts as they plummeted. The table, chairs, students, and the teacher came to a stop. The word Siseneg appeared on the table, revealing which floor (book) they had travelled to via the class table elevator.

"Blimey! What was that?" Beck looked around in startled wonderment.

Mrs. Good looked over her startled children. "That Mr. Comrade is the classroom elevator. It can travel to every book in the main Academy building; simply draw the name of the room you wish to visit and it will transfer you there."

Lots of "Cools" and "Wows" echoed from the students. Xander and Beck grinned wickedly. Even though they had just met, they were all little boys who loved the thrill of high speeds and making their mothers swoon. They were both considering what would happen if they never stopped writing on the table. Imagine how the elevator would zoom up and down endlessly.

"Does it go left and right?" the boys asked each other. Mrs. Good looked consternated. She replied with a very quick "No" and turned away.

The book room they had entered via the classroom elevator contained fifty smaller rooms, all accessible from the dead center of the main room, where the elevator stopped.

"Children, please proceed to room 1. The rooms are labelled at the top of the door so you won't get confused. Oh dear boy, what's wrong?" Mrs. Good asked Drew, who looked pale and held his hands over his mouth.

"He can't handle the ride!" Marstin cackled to his friends. The tall and lanky Roy teased his younger, more rotund brother. They laughed, bumped into each other, and snorted.

"Enough of that, boys," scolded Mrs. Good. Go on and study in the rooms there; I will take Mr. Drew to the infirmary. Behave!" And with a SWOOSH! They disappeared upward.

Tarah and Lucy moved into the room labeled Chapter 1. Marstin and his cronies, of course, ran through each room, yelling and wailing.

Tarah huffed at Xander, "See Xander right here. It answers your question." Xander and Beck entered the room.

"Mama, she's annoying," mumbled Beck. The room was filled with writings. It felt like you had stepped into a book. On the walls were ancient verses etched into the grey stonewalls in bold-faced perfect cursive lettering. Beginning with 1, it went in a circle and stopped at 31.

"Look!" exclaimed Tarah, pointing to verse 1. "It clearly states that the Master created everything, including us." Alexander approached the wall slowly, tracing his hand over the lettering. He noticed that the first letter of the first word wasn't indented but was sticking out. Curious, Xander reached out and pushed on it.

The walls suddenly shuddered, and bits of stone dribbled around the group and before them, a small opening revealed itself as the wall slid sideways.

Xander glanced around. The girls looked petrified, and poor Beck looked like he was about to faint. "Come on! Hurry! Before Mrs. Good comes back", Xander grabbed Beck, Tarah, and Lucy fell in behind, huddling up as close as they could, as they walked into the pitch-black room.

# Chapter 4
# Light And Dark

"Where's the light?" whispered Beck.

"I don't know. Check for a candle or a switch," said Xander, as they groped along the walls. But before they could make any progress, they heard a sinister, dark, and creepy voice that sounded like a snake. The voice said, "Behold, am I not as great as thee? Give me thy power, and I shall rule!"

A deep, soft voice replied, "I gave you all your desires, but that I cannot give. Depart from me."

The children were startled as bright flashing lights of all colors suddenly flashed in their direction and hurled at the students, causing them to flinch in unison.

Abruptly, someone grabbed them and dragged them out of the darkness, back to Chapter 1. Mrs. Good looked angry and instructed the four of them to board the table platform. They hurriedly buckled up and were suddenly lifted up and to the right. Each floor had a passage that connected them.

They entered a tranquil study where a soft fire crackled. The room was adorned with manuscripts, paintings, and unique objects from around the world.

In the center, a vast wooden desk was situated. Behind it were big, tall windows backlighting the desk. Behind the papers and a medieval-looking lamp sat a long-bearded man with spectacles and neatly combed brown hair. His straight black suit was ironed perfectly crisp. He peered over the desk at them.

"Ah, Mrs. Good, what brings you here?" He inquired.

Mrs. Good huffed, "I found these four students in one of the dark rooms, Head Minister."

The head minister raised his eyebrows. "Very well. If you please leave them with me, I will see that they return. Come forward, boys and girls."

The children shuffled sheepishly towards the head minister as Mrs. Good bowed her head briefly before exiting.

"So, tell me, children. Which dark room did you visit?"

Xander spoke up, "We didn't mean to Sir, honestly. We just…"

The head minister raised his hand to reassure the children, "Don't worry, you're not in trouble." He smiled as he noticed the children visibly relax. "All rooms are open to all students, but the dark rooms are usually reserved for older students who can comprehend what they see. Do you understand what you saw?"

Beck, Lucy, Tarah, and Xander all shook their heads.

The head minister smiled, "That's okay." He folded his hands on his desk, "Now, which room was it?"

Tarah answered, "Book Siseneg, Room 1."

Head Minister nodded, "Ah, the first uprising."

"What happened, Sir? What did we see? Whose voices did we hear?" blurted Beck.

The head minister took a moment to gather his thoughts before speaking, "What you just heard was the first battle between good and evil. At the Academy, we teach our students how to fight the darkness that exists within each of us. If we're not careful, this darkness can consume us." He sat up straight and looked at each of them, "In the beginning, before time itself, The Master had many servants who were devoted to him. However, his head servant, Moerasthom, became power-hungry and wanted to replace The Master. This was the voice you heard. As a result, The Master cast Moerasthom and those who followed him in the rebellion into the fires of darkness." The head minister paused, observing their horrified expressions.

"Wh-where is he now?" stammered Beck.

The head minister patted his shoulder, "I'm getting to that part. Because of him, we now all bear his dark, treacherous ways in us, but as for where he is, he could be anywhere. Not all who are born and raised as Light Followers continue and strive for the Master. Be wary and NEVER let your guard down."

"And where is the Master?" Xander wondered.

"Well, for now, The Master is traveling; however, he is due any day now."

Lucy's blue eyes clouded in consternation, "But how will we know it is him?" she asked.

The head minister smiled and said, "The best way for you young ones to recognize him is by looking for his pure white horse with two big white wings and flashing eyes. He will come flying to the sound of a very loud trumpet."

The grandfather clock loudly donged, proclaiming the hour. The Head Minister took note of it. Returning his gaze to the children, he said, "Enough for now. Why don't you go back to Mrs. Good? I have writings to prepare. Quickly now, back to the table!"

The children stood in astonishment, for there was the exact class table Mrs. Good had used when she left.

The Head Minister chuckled at their amazement, "Don't seem so surprised. It is not the same table but one of 85 identical tables. You see, there is one for each floor, and when you travel to another level, all the tables switch with the room above or below them. So, if I were you, I would not study at the class table." He smiled again in wry humor.

"Eighty-five? But there's only sixty-six floors", Tarah interjected. The minister smiled again, "So there is young Miss. Now, Alexander, take the Teachers teacher's seat, and the rest of you strap up. When you are ready Alexander draw with your finger MLR1 for Main Level Room 1. And I do hope you all have a wonderful time."

## Light And Dark

Xander drew the letters on the tabletop, and away they zoomed to the left, then up.

# Chapter 5
# The Games

As they clunked to a stop at their classroom, Drew awaited them impatiently. "There you guys are. Come on, where were you anyway? Never mind, they are about to start. Hurry up!" He dashed out the door.

The group followed, running through the main hall, taking a right past the girls' room, and out into the covered walk to the right-side dorms.

The Academy had many large open areas covered with green bushes and grass, which the children loved to play and have fun. On one side of the fields were tall redwood trees with circumferences of ten to thirty feet that reached up to the sky. These trees had sprawling root systems that created hollows and perfect hiding places for games like 'Where's My Sheep' and 'One O'clock the Wolf is Here.'

To the north lie the Swamps of Hate, known for their treacherous terrain consisting of mud bogs, quicksand, tall, dry grasses, monstrous serpents, alligators, and countless mosquitoes. Whoever ventures into these swamps must be prepared to face the perils of the Dark Work of Hate, as everything in these swamps is dangerous and deadly.

To the west, eight-foot neatly trimmed shrub bushes are aligned in a row. Anyone can approach the whiteboard erected nearby between two upright posts deeply sunk into the earth for stability in windy times. One can grab the marking quill and draw whatever design, shape, symbol, maze, or map they desire. As soon as the drawing is finished, the shrubs will twist and rotate forty times to match the exact design.

Academy teachers had the privilege of punishing disobedient students by making them solve mazes. The teacher would draw the mazes on the whiteboard, and the students had to find their way out.

## The Games

However, the teacher would not help the students until they learned their lesson. Often, it would take so long that by the time the students found their way out, it would be dark outside, and they would be completely lost.

Of course, to the south lies the Academy, with its ten dorm buildings jutting out to the sides and curving around their roundabouts.

Fruit trees grew between the dorms, supplying the occupants with juicy fresh fruits during blossom time.

In the grass field, there was a symmetrical cross measuring twenty feet from outside to outside corner and from outside corner to inside corner. One arm of the cross was equal to a twenty-by-twenty square. The game of tag played was complex. Five teams participated, four of which stood on the four sides of the cross. Each team had a base, and players had to stay on their baseline to remain safe. If they stepped off the baseline, any player from the opposing team could catch them. If a player were caught, they would be out until the end of the round. If the player who tagged them was caught, they could re-enter the game. In the center of the cross was a circle resembling a crown of thorns, with a key resting in a holder. The game's objective was to retrieve the key without being caught and return safely to the base. The team that retrieved the key was declared the winner. If a player with the key was caught, the key returned to the center ring stand. A player could throw the key to a teammate before being tagged. If the key landed on the ground, it would return to the center. Every team aimed to snatch the key from the stand or intercept a throw. The fifth team's goal was to guard the key for sixteen minutes. Their base was the circle surrounding the key and its stand. They switched out teams if they successfully guarded the key for sixteen minutes. This cycle could repeat for three rounds. If the key was defended successfully by any or all the teams selected to protect it for all rounds, the match ended, and no team won. However, if a team retrieved the key, the game ended, and the victorious team kept the key. The first team to collect three keys could submit them to the Head Principal Carethemost, who would transport them to The Coliseum.

Alexander, Beck, Tarah, and Lucy started towards the other students standing by the outlined cross in the field. "What are they wearing," Beck Asked, staring intently ahead and shielding his eyes against the blinding sun.

"It looks as if they have on some kind of uniform" "replied Xander, following his gaze and squinting to better focus his eyes.

"Hey, you four," interrupted Mrs. Good, "Go immediately to your dormitory and put on your uniforms. They are in your room's wardrobe. Chop Chop! Hurry Now!" She shooed them away with her hands turned around and stomped towards the other gathered children.

"Chop Chop," Beck mimicked in a squeaking voice with his hands on his hips; returning to his normal voice, he said, "Make me, you chop chop," and he made a twisted tongue face and stuck it towards her.

The others laughed. "Come on, let's go." Xander pulled Beck toward their dorm. Lucy and Tarah were already hurrying toward their rooms.

As they entered the room, Beck flopped on his bed,, which was the bottom bunk, while Xander slept above him. "Ugh, I'm tired. I don't want to play any stupid game," he huffed. Alexander ignored his friends' whining and went to the wardrobe by one of the two windows in their room. Pulling open the door, he glanced inside. Seeing their game uniforms, he grabbed them both, turning and throwing one on Beck.

"Umph," Beck muttered. Then he held up his uniform for inspection: "Green and white stripes with black breeches."

Xander glanced at Beck, and he started pulling off his school uniform. "Yes! Beck, to match our straws and Earth dorm. "Now, would you hurry up and get dressed already?". Slowly, Beck started to follow suit.

# The Games

Once ready, they stepped outside. Tarah and Lucy stood waiting for them in fully matching green and white striped dresses with black socks.

"Nice Socks", Beck teased.

Tarah glared, "I'd say whoever invented these hateful things needs to be dismembered." Alexander and Beck cackled boyishly. Lucy glanced at them, "Well, I think we all look charming. Now let's go".

They ran for the group of students, arriving just in time to hear the gamekeeper, Maximus, say, "So those are the rules. Remember, No going out of bounds, or you are out of the game for the day." He turned to the arriving four as they approached, "You're late. We do not have time to waste. Just ask someone the rules as you play or watch and learn." He turned to the rest of the group, rubbing his hands together, and said, "Okay now, to the spinner!"

The cross was positioned at the cardinal points of north, east, south, and west. In the southeast corner, a large needle was spun to determine the center defending team for the first three minutes.

"Everyone, everyone!" Maximus said, "If I can have you all separate into your dorm colors, please." The children started separating, pushing past each other to get to their teammates. "Very good." Maximus continued once everyone was separated. "Okay, now I will spin the needle." He reached down, grasping the spinning needle with two large hands, for he was quite a large barrel of a man. He slowly twisted back and forth as the students gathered around, trying to get as close as possible. Maximus heaved the needle and jumped out of the way as it spun ferociously in a circle. It spun for a while, then slowly stopped, pointing at yellow.

Maximus gestured towards the students belonging to the Air dormitory and assigned them their respective positions. "The yellow team will be positioned in the center, the Green team in the North, the Red team in the East, the Gray team in the South, and the Blue team in the West. We will begin on my mark." Maximus then climbed up to a raised wooden platform where he could oversee and judge the game.

Once everyone had been assigned, he said, "Get ready, set, go!" and blew a loud horn whistle. Everyone jumped into action. Henry gestured to Alexander and Beck, "Be careful and watch when others leave their base. Keep an eye on me, and I'll signal if I need your help." And with that, he trotted towards the middle. Alexander and Beck took a running stance with one foot in front and the other on their baseline. Students chased each other around. A boy named Dodger dove for the key but was caught in midair by Beck's sister Sally. Students who were eliminated stood on the sidelines, cheering their teammates on.

An older boy left his base to watch as the center defender. Alexander saw his opportunity and ran for him. Weaving in and out and around other players, dodging right and left as he reached to tag his back. Wham! The world spun as Xander flew through the air, spinning and landing, Meeting the earth violently. Dizzy and reeling, he looked up. Marstin stood over him, sneering, "Ha! That's what you get, worm! Enjoy the sidelines, runt!" He pranced, laughing and looking around to ensure people saw his victory.

Lucy and Beck ran over. "Xander, are you alright?" Beck asked as they reached down, helped him to his feet, and brushed him off.

Alexander nodded, "Yeah, Yeah, I'm fine. Just a little sore. That guy is a tank! Mamma, that hurt!" They walked to the edge, where their other teammates waited. "Are you guys out, too?" he asked Beck and Lucy.

Lucy replied, "Yeah, we were caught straight away."

As time passed, teams lost and gained players until the horn sounded to notify the students that the round had ended.

"Alright, everyone, switch in a clockwise fashion. The north team moves to the east, the east team moves to the south, and so on. West team, you will go to the Defenders center." The gamekeeper held his horn to his lips again, "WOOOOOOOOO!" The horn sounded again, and the game continued.

## The Games

Alexander managed to eliminate two other players but sadly was eliminated at the end of the second round. Lucy eliminated a player, but poor Beck was mobbed at the beginning of the game and was eliminated immediately. Tarah was a very effective dodger but lacked the speed to catch anyone. On the other hand, Henry was excellent at running, dodging, and catching. In the third round, when everyone had rotated, he almost singlehandedly won the game when he stole the key and ran for their team base, but as it happened, Alexander, who was in front of him, tripped, causing Henry to swerve right into the defenders' path who eliminated him grabbing the key and returning it to the center.

Henry's fellow dormers ran over, "Ugh, these kids are worthless!" Another one ran past them and muttered, "What a skinny kid, can't run for nothing."

Henry shook his head, "Come on, guys. I am fine. We will try again." He looked at Alexander and offered him a hand, "It's all good, bud. Not to worry. It's just your first time playing." He smiled and rushed off to the sidelines, leaving Tara, Lucy, Beck, and Xander.

Lucy giggled, "Oh, he's so dreamy!"

"And handsome, too," Tara finished for her. The girls giggled and blushed together.

Beck rolled his eyes, "Oh, for Pete's sake. You girls are gross".

Alexander walked back to base his mind in turmoil. Why did he have to trip? What was wrong with him? Why was he always messing up? It seemed he could not get anything right ever.

At the end of the game, the grey team successfully retrieved the key. Alexander and his three friends watched as Marstin held the key aloft and jeered at everyone else loudly, whooping with his friends over their victory.

"I can't believe it! He didn't even score the winning goal. It was that boy over there," Tara pointed her head towards a younger boy standing alone on the side. Even though the team's victory was all thanks to him, no one congratulated him. "You take that back," Beck growled in response.

Beck spat, "He is just a low-down attention grabber that is all." He turned to Alexander, but Xander was already walking alone towards the dorm. His head was high, but his heart felt heavy and cold.

Lucy called out to him, "Xander, wait up!" The three started running towards him, "We don't think it's your fault."

"Yeah, none of us do." Beck glared at Tara, who was opening her mouth to contradict him. Instead, she closed her mouth and nodded in agreement.

Xander looked at them and tried to smile. "Thanks, guys, but let's just go to our next lesson." He turned and walked inside. His three friends glanced at each other, not knowing what to say to convince Xander it was not his fault. Shrugging, they followed Alexander into the schoolhouse a little slower.

# Chapter 6
# The Head Council

Headmaster Carethemost observed the game from his classroom, watching the pupils engage wholeheartedly. He smiled, resting his hands on the windowsill, and suddenly, he turned as if remembering something. He strolled to the class table, tracing the letters PTLC, and in a flash, he flew off down and to the left, traveling for some time before coming to a stop inside a dimly lit room with a small door adjoining this small room to a larger one.

The headmaster walked to the door. Engraved on it was the single word "job.". He spoke to the door, "Thirty-one dot dot Thirty-Two." The door immediately creaked open, revealing a table with twelve chairs surrounding it. Eleven of the chairs were already filled. He stepped into the oval-shaped room. Twelve pillars encircled the table, paintings of saints lined the walls, and lights fixed on the wall reflected light onto the table, revealing the men's stern faces.

No windows allowed outside light to penetrate. On the long black table lay manuscripts, books, scrolls, and literature from around the globe. Large volumes sat behind the men on shelves fixated between the white pillars.

A man at the head of the table twisted to look at Carethemost. The man was in his ancient years with a long beard that was white as snow, and his hair matched his beard. A straight black suit adorned him. After studying Carethemost for a brief moment, he spoke, "Headmaster, we were just about to start."

Carethemost inclined his head slightly towards the older man. "Yes, I'm sorry, I have little time today, but I have important news, Head Bishop."

Head Bishop motioned to the empty chair and said, "Please sit down and tell us your news." Carethmost nodded at the other three masters, four deacons, and four ministers, including the head minister, who spoke to Alexander and his friends. And finally, the three remaining bishops.

He then seated himself and spoke, "He's here." The men's eyes all opened wide, and everyone began to whisper and mutter among themselves.

"Silence." Everyone looked to the Head Bishop, who was standing. "When did he arrive, and why was I not notified?" He asked, looking at each man and finally landing on Carethemost.

Carethemost answered, "It's my fault, sir; I did not know he was to arrive this term."

"Not to worry. Does anyone else know?" Head Bishop sat back down, waiting for the answer from Carethemost, who shook his head. "Only us in this room and his mother. His Father passed shortly after his birth."

"Some of us don't know what is going on." A short, newly ordained deacon spoke up.

The Head Bishop, whose name is Amatus (which translates to Beloved), motioned to two of the men, "Check the doors and lock them." He turned toward the short deacon. "This boy we speak of is to be a great leader for us in the dark years ahead when the soul snatcher..." He paused as the men glanced around at each other. "Tries to crush us again. He tried in the beginning as Moecrasethon, then again when the Son of Light came. Now that the boy is of age, we know the time draws near again. The master has always promised his protection. If this boy is to lead us, we must guide him and watch him closely; it's only a matter of time before the soul snatcher discovers he is of age and here at the academy." He looked to Carethmost and said, "So... Which one is he?"

Carethemost gave a brief description of the boy in question as all the men listened intently.

Head minister Segundo looked at Carethemost and said, "Mrs. Good brought him to me today and his three friends." He returned his gaze to Amatus. "He's an intense little fellow with dark, inquisitive eyes, but I sense he is unsure and a little shy. Maybe we should inform him of his future calling."

Amatus stared at the table silently. Then, to the council, he offered a suggestion: "Maybe we will in time, but for now, let's let him grow and mature in the works of light." The eleven men surrounding him all nodded in agreement.

Carethemost glanced at his timepiece. "Excuse me, gentlemen. I have lessons to teach; do stop by and visit if you get the chance." He stood, making his way towards the door from which he entered.

"Oh, and Carethmost," Amatus called out. Carethmost turned briefly to look towards the Head Bishop. "Do look after the boy, and on a side note, if you see Dr. Skane, send him our way if you please. We would like to have a few words with him." Carethemost raised his eyebrows in silent question. "We have reports he has been spreading heresies, and we would like to know the story directly from him." Amatus finished.

Carethemost bowed, "Of course, sir, as you wish. Goodbye for now." He closed the door and stepped to the table, tracing his finger once again on the table and spelling out the letters MLR4.

# Chapter 7
# Poisoned

Mrs. Good stepped into the classroom, and the children's laughter and merrymaking died out. They all quickly assumed their desks in an orderly fashion. Mrs. Good glared from student to student. "Who can tell me what the Dark Work of Deception means?" She looked around her classroom as they all sat there quietly, avoiding her gaze, hoping to be unnoticed. Her eyes landed on Beck, and her eyes narrowed. Beck glanced up and quickly tried to pretend he was putting a lot of thought into her question, "Mr. Comrade." She pointed a finger towards Beck.

Beck looked up quickly, stuttering, "Umm, yes, ma'am?"

"What does it mean?" She asked again.

Beck shook his head. "I'm not exactly sure." He stammered. Mrs. Good glared long and hard at him. Lucy came to his rescue: "It means to lie or to make someone believe something that isn't true." Mrs. Good turned her hard gaze towards Lucy, who shrunk behind Alexander, regretting her decision to come to Beck's rescue.

Mrs. Good finally nodded. "Correct. Now. I want a descriptive six-hundred-word essay written by tomorrow afternoon." Everyone simultaneously groaned. "Silence!" She snapped. "You may use the elevator to study at any level. I need not remind you what happens if you don't finish on time." She let her eyes roam over the group, who all sat there trying to hide the annoyance that was threatening to show on their faces. "Now, off with you. Dismissed!" Waving her hands towards the children, she stacked her books and then walked out of the room.

"Jingle bells," whispered Beck. "That woman scares me.".

"Me too," Lucy put in, "I thought she was going to punish me for answering Beck's question."

Beck lightly tapped her arm with his book. "Yeah, thanks for saving me, Lucy.".

Lucy looked down shyly and said, "You're welcome. She's a brute." By this time, children were rushing to the table to be off to their studies, but Marstin and his crew pushed and knocked others aside and claimed the table for themselves.

"Us first, you milksops," Marstin gave his typical sneer, pushing Drew off the platform. "Use the stairs or just wait for us to be done; either way, we don't care." They all guffawed and slapped each other on the back as they disappeared into the ceiling. Another table came onto the site, and others piled on, selecting their level and speeding off.

Alexander, Beck, and Lucy huddled around the cheat sheet for the elevator book rooms. In the cheat sheet it had the name of each level and an outline of what information each level contained.

"Let's go back to Siseneg. I remember reading something about someone being deceived," Lucy suggested.

"Ok. Let's go. We will take your word for it," Alexander agreed, closing the cheat sheet booklet. He looked over at Tara, who was sitting at the window in a trance-like stare. Her books spread out on the windowsill as she stared outside. "Tara, are you coming with us?" He called over to her. She blinked as if she had just awakened and spun towards them.

"Sure," she said, walking towards them unsteadily, swaying slightly. Beck grabbed her arm before she fell and studied her face. "You, okay?" He asked with just a hint of worry lacing his voice.

Tara nodded. "Yes, yeah, I'm fine. I must have stood up too fast." She pulled her arm back and looked at Alexander. "Where are we headed?" She asked as they walked over to the chairs and started buckling in. Beck followed a bit slower, still studying Tara.

"We are going back to level one," Alexander replied while he wrote on the table board. "Hang on," he warned as they took off abruptly. After traveling swiftly for a moment, they came to a stop at the bottom.

"Whew," Beck whistled, grinning, "I won't ever get sick of that feeling."

"Do ya'll ever wonder where all you can go on this elevator?" Lucy asked while attempting to fix her hair that was frizzed all over her face.

Beck, still grinning, replied, "I'll bet it goes to the moon."

"Don't be silly, Beck," Tara scolded. "It only travels to places that directly affect the academy and its assets."

Beck scowled at her for disagreeing: "Take the moon away, and I'd bet that would affect the academy and its assets." He mocked her last words by emphasizing them.

Tara glared at him and huffed, "You're horrid." She fell over her shoulder as she started stomping away.

"And you're a goody goody two shoes who thinks she knows it all," Beck called after her right on her heels. They were so busy arguing and walking that they bumped into Xander and Lucy, who were in room three.

"Look!" Lucy exclaimed, pointing, "right there. The first few verses are just where I thought." Alexander smiled and said, "Excellent." He walked to the wall, examining the letters carefully.

"Alexander, no, not again," Beck moaned, rubbing his hands across his face dramatically. "I mean, if you happen upon a dark room, that's one thing, but don't go looking for them." He walked over and pulled on Xander's tunic.

"Ah ha, I found it," Xander triumphantly stated. "See right there in the third verse, it sticks out." Beck grabbed Xander, and the girls looked frightened as they all cried in unison. "Don't touch it!!"

"The last time was so scary," Lucy whimpered. A mischievous gleam entered Xander's eyes, and his mouth quirked in a grin.

## Poisoned

"Oh, I hate that look," Beck moaned again as Alexander pushed in the letter G. The floor tumbled and shook. Dust flew as the walls groaned. A roar erupted. The room shook. Someone screamed. Then, as suddenly as the shaking started, it stopped.

Beck peeked through his fingers that were tightly held over his face and said, "That wasn't so bad." He wiped his hands on his trousers. He looked over at Xander, who had a strange look on his face. "What?" He asked.

Xander grinned, "Did you say..." Suddenly, the floor beneath their feet gave way, and they plummeted into the darkness below them. This time, all four of them screamed in unison as they descended further into the mirky blackness.

"Ugh, I'm going to be sick," Beck called out. Alexander grabbed his hand, yelling, "So we don't get separated." He grabbed Lucy with his other hand, and Beck followed his lead, reaching out and grabbing Tara's outstretched hand. Suddenly, light appeared as they landed in the softest, most lush grass they had ever felt. They all sat up, slowly looking around in shocked bewilderment.

Surrounding them were mighty fruit trees and beautiful flowers of blue, yellow, red, and white. A gentle breeze ruffled their hair as a feeling of love and happiness hung in the air. In the distance, they could see a beautiful waterfall cascading down a rock cliff that had wildflowers covering it. Brooks giggled as they swept through the land, falling gently over rocks of all colors that made up the waterbed. Beautiful birds of all colors flew ahead, calling to each other as they played an entertaining game of tag. Lions, deer, elephants, foxes, and elk, along with lots of other animals—so many that the children couldn't process—all grazed in a field nearby. None of them seemed frightened by the fact that predators were among them.

Not far from where they sat grew a majestic tree with the most delicious-looking fruit hanging from its branches.

The four of them stood there in awe, taking in all the sights and sounds, holding their breath for fear of ruining the majestic work of art that was alive in front of them.

Beck and Tara both looked down at their hands, which were still tightly gripping each other. They both yanked their hands-free. Tara blushed as Beck wiped his hands on his trousers, muttering to himself.

Suddenly, Lucy grabbed Xander. "I know where we are," she exclaimed excitedly. "We are in the garden where darkness entered the world in the very beginning!" As she spoke, a woman approached the large, majestic tree.

Movement in the tree drew their attention. They heard a sugary, raspy voice speak with a cunning, convincing manner, "Die if you eat? Nay, but ye shall be rulers of all," the voice tempted. The woman, so beguiled and convinced by the voice, took the fruit and slowly took a bite, then disappeared into the surrounding trees.

"Wait. What happened?" Beck asked, trying to look further into the trees.

"The serpent just deceived man to bring sin and works of darkness into the world. The Master then banishes them from the garden," Lucy explained.

"So that's why we are born in darkness," Tara put in. "Come on, the Master comes and talks to them. Let's go see him." She stopped and looked down as she felt a tug on her feet. She looked around at the others. They were all looking down because they could feel it.

Suddenly, they were all sucked into the ground. Tara screamed as they fell through blurring gray lights and were plunked unceremoniously into the room they had previously started in. Tara stood, adjusting her skirt angrily. She glared at Alexander and said, "You and your dumb button pushing." She spat, "I am just plum sick and tired of it all."

## Poisoned

Xander tried to look remorseful. "I'm sorry, Tara. I'll try to warn you next time."

"Next time? NEXT TIME?" Tara shouted towards him, "There won't be a next time!"

"But don't you see we can discover so much more in the dark rooms so much faster?" He looked around at each of his friends. "Weeks ago, we found out about the Soulsnatcher being banished, and now we see how he came in the form of a serpent and deceived mankind, poisoning everyone with the Dark Works. We're much farther ahead. Now, six hundred words on deception will be a breeze. And" He held up his hand toward Tara as she started opening her mouth to interrupt his reasoning. "And remember how the head minister warned us about how the soul snatcher could be anywhere? Now we know he can be in the form of a snake.

"He's kind of got a point, you know," Beck pointed out.

"Well, fine," Tara huffed. "But you boys better get your writing done, or you won't get any help from us," Tara stomped out of the room. Lucy grinned as she turned to go. She grabbed Xander's sleeve and said, "Please get your essay done. You don't want to have to clean the girl's bathroom again." And with that, she ran out the door with the sounds of Alexander's protests and Beck's laughter ringing in her ears.

### Dr. Skane

"Dr Skane!" Head Bishop Amatus' call silenced the Council: "You are accused of heresy and publishing that which would turn people away from the light. What do you have to say against these accusations?" He looked at the man in question.

Dr. Skane looked at the Council and gathered his thoughts before he made his statement, "Who here has not said rash things or an idea that was or could have been misleading? I truly am sorry, gentlemen, if I have offended or misled anyone. It is true that I did say things that were untrue, but I retraced my steps and have apologized to the people I have offended and misled. As for publishing, I have not published any dark works. But I am open to your punishment as you see fit, Council." He bowed his head and prepared for the worst. Everyone was aware of the Council and their haste to make judgments at times.

The council members began to argue and mutter amongst themselves. "I feel as though we should excommunicate him. Lying and heresies are not something we want in our Light Followers congregation, as they could lead others astray even though he has apologized. Once he has shown true repentance and has not continued to do these things, we can bring him back into the fold," Carethemost stated.

"But he was honest and straightforward." A young deacon, Jhos, fired back.

"We can't trust him," Segundo muttered.

"I vote to give him a period of reform," Bishop Sophron reasoned.

"But then we will have to watch him, and I don't know about you, but I am busy enough." Another put in slapping his hands on the table.

"Enough," Amatus' voice echoed through the council room. "I suggest we send him to the academy," Dr. Skane said, raising his head in hope as the council came alive. Some are outraged, and others are in agreement. Amatus raised his hand, and they all stopped speaking. "I don't suggest any interaction with the students. He shall help Maximus with the grounds, cleaning up after the carrier pigeons, and general maintenance. All under the supervision of my good friend Headmaster Carethemost," Amatus nodded at the Head Master. The Council considered their options carefully, every man weighing the consequences and outcomes of different avenues. All were perplexed and unable to come up with any better ideas. Amatus, let them mull the problem in their heads for a moment. The clock ticked steadily in the corner.

# Poisoned

Dr. Skane shifted from one foot to the other at the end of the table, where he stood, looking very apprehensive. After what seemed to Dr. Skane to be hours but was, in fact, only a matter of a few minutes, Amatus spoke, "We will all vote on it. I will bow out due to the fact that it was my idea. All in favor of sending Dr. Skane to AGE to help on the grounds, please raise your hand."

Seven men raised their hands, including Jhos and Sophron. Amatus glanced at Carethemost and said, "Good luck, my friend." Then, looking at Dr. Skane, he said, "This is a second chance. I expect you won't take it for granted or treat it lightly."

Dr. Skane stood there trembling, looking like the weight of the world was just lifted off his shoulders. "No, sir! Thank you very much!" He bowed to the council and started backpedaling towards the exit for fear the council would change their mind.

Amatus nodded. "Very well. Head Master, please show Dr. Skane to his lodging quarters and give this letter to Alexander." He handed a piece of paper wrapped in twine to Carethemost and said, "Thank you, gentlemen, that will be all for today."

**********************

"Who is that man with Mr. Skane?" Beck asked Lucy and Xander as the dorms gathered for another game of Begotten. The breeze blew softly, rustling the trees as the smell of oncoming winter filled the air.

Lucy shivered against the wind as she pulled her coat closer around her. "I heard from Drew, who heard from Henry, who was sneaking around and saw Mr. CaretheMost bring him up through the elevator and show him to some rooms, saying something about it being his living quarters in the teacher's dorm." She took a deep breath, realizing somewhere in her haste to share what she knew, she forgot to breathe.

Alexander looked up from tying his shoes at the man in question. He shivered as the gray-haired man turned and smiled directly at him, nodding his head and slightly raising a hand. Xander quickly dropped his head back to his shoes, a feeling of unease rushing through him, although he couldn't figure out why. He shook his head, telling himself that it was just the breeze that made him feel a bit cold.

"Did you tell them yet?" Beck questioned Xander.

Tarah looked up from a book she was reading. "Tell us what?" She snapped towards the boys.

"Hey, don't look at me. It was Alexander who got the letter. Why do you have a book out on the field, Miss Snob? We are getting ready to play, not study." Beck said defensively.

Tara bristled, "Snob? I'll let you know I am not snobby! And I am allowed to read anywhere, please."

"Whatever you say," Beck waited until Tara went back to reading her book, apparently forgetting the questions she had posed to Xander, "Miss Touchy." He muttered and bolted off across the field. Tara dropped her book and sped after him, hot on his trail, intent on wounding him.

Alexander and Lucy laughed as they watched their fighting comrades weave in and out of other players who were on the field waiting for the match to begin. Lucy turned to Xander and asked, "What letter?"

Xander shook his head. "It's nothing, just a letter the head bishop gave to me.".

Lucy's eyes widened. "What does it say?"

Alexander shrugged. "I don't know; I haven't actually opened it yet."

"What? Why Not? It's from the Head Bishop." She said his name emphatically, "It's got to be important.".

Alexander sighed. "You ask a bloody lot of questions, but if you really must know, it's from my father. He wrote it for me before he died, so I'm not sure I really want to read it." He smiled half-heartedly at Lucy. She gave him a small smile back, trying her best to understand his reasoning.

Just then, a voice rang out, "Alright! Teams at the ready." Maximus stood at the edge of the outlined cross, his hands held above his head, a whistle in his mouth at the ready. Everyone ran to their bases and aligned themselves according to each of their designated positions on the team. Once all defenses were in place, a shrill whistle echoed across the field as Maximus threw his arms down, motioning the beginning of the game. Dr. Skane yelled, "START.".

In the final round, Alexander took off, running towards the defense in the middle. He dodged right as a big hand swooped towards him. Immediately, he dove left into the middle circle base surrounding the key. Grabbing it, he ran toward his base. Lucy and Henry were yelling out warnings to him, encouraging him and alerting him to other teammates intent on taking him out. With only a few minutes left until this round, Xander was determined to get this key for his team.

His lungs burned, and his legs ached as he swerved back and forth, avoiding other taggers. Suddenly, he tripped, falling flat, his face meeting the dirt. Marstin laughed and tagged him gleefully, "Now give me the key, whittle boy!" He mocked.

Alexander rolled over, smiling as he opened his hand. It was empty. Marstin glared sourly, looking around on the ground for the dropped key. Hearing whooping, he looked up, seeing Beck on base hooting and waving the key. When Alexander tripped, the key flowed out of his hand. Beck, who was waiting as Xander's backup, had seen it fly into the air and had caught it, taking it home to claim the victory for the Earth Team.

Marstin blinked angrily and huffed as he pushed Alexander as he was trying to stand up, making Xander fall into the dirt again.

"Worm, get out of my way or be trampled," Marstin yelled and stomped off.

"Young Man!" A firm voice made Marstin turn wide-eyed at an upset Mr. Skane, who was strolling rapidly to his side. He grabbed Marstin by the ear and said, "Let's see what the headmaster says about your behavior." He proceeded to drag Marstin by his ear towards the academy's double doors.

Students came running to Alexander. Beck placed the key in his hand and thumped him on the back. "We did it, Alex," he stated excitedly, barely catching his breath even now. He offered a hand to Xander to help him stand up.

Xander smiled in triumph, taking Beck's hand and raising it to his feet. "You did it, Beck. Great catch." The other students chimed in with words of praise and congratulations. Henry weaved his way through the festive cheering crowd to where the boys were standing, holding the key.

"Well done, boys, very well done." He clapped them on their shoulders and said, "Another step farther away from choir singing!"

Beck looked up at him incredulously and said, "Wait, wait! Whatcha mean choir singing?" He gulped loudly, suddenly looking like he could possibly toss up his lunch.

"Oh, you know. We play Begotten all year, and then at the end of the term, the winners get to go to the Colosseum, while the team with the least number of keys must sing for the middle teams and all the parents. A sort of program, you see." Alex and Beck's eyes widened in horror as they looked at Henry, trying to decipher if he was joking. Henry laughed at their expression. "But don't worry, guys, just keep playing like you did today, and you'll be golden." He thumped them both on the back again and said, "See you in the grand hall."

Beck turned toward Xander, a horrified expression still pasted on his face. "Singing! Singing?!" He exploded. "What kind of human torture is that?"

# Poisoned

Xander shrugged. "I don't know, but I bet it's against the Geneva Convention for sure." He shook his head, telling himself they had better not lose. Lucy and Tara finally made it over to their side through all the merrymakers.

The crowd started making their way towards the Academy building to celebrate with a feast in the Grand Hall. As they walked, Lucy jumped up and said, "I think I like Dr. Skane. He sure showed Marstin who is boss." They all laughed, remembering how Marstin had been unceremoniously transported across the yard on his tippytoes.

"Maybe now he won't bully you," Tara giggled.

Xander grinned. "Yeah, but sadly, he will probably just be more discreet about it when no teacher is around. Maybe your right, Tara, but I still don't get his pick with me, though." Alexander looked thoughtfully confused.

Lucy tried to cheer him back up, saying, "Don't think about him. He's just an old toad." She assured him.

"I suppose you're right. I just must be careful not to give him any chances to get even." Xander tried to look confident. "At least I have you guys at my back.".

Beck grinned and, through an arm over Xander's shoulder, said, "You always got us here. Now let's forget him and enjoy tonight's victory! We WON!". Beck swung open the double doors as they got up to them. The sound of cheers and yelling came from inside as they saw him and Alexander walk in. Beck smiled in triumph as they walked to their seats. Never had they felt so important.

# Chapter 8
# The Letter

Alexander crawled into his bed. He could hear the older students still enjoying their time celebrating. He smiled, looking at the key that Henry had graciously placed in his and Beck's dorm rooms. It nestled on a shelf in the corner. Beck, who had given up a scarf for it to lay on, now snored happily under Alexander in his bottom bunk, dreaming of fame and glory.

Drew and Jonathan had separate beds on the other side of the room and were sleeping peacefully as well, or so Xander hoped. He quietly unfolded the letter he had tucked under his pillow, lighting a small candle. He shaded it as best he could so he wouldn't disturb his sleeping roommates. He took a deep breath and started reading.

"Son, I lay here dying, wishing I could be there for you as the time comes, but since that is impossible, I'm writing this letter, hoping it helps prepare you for your future.

Your mother and I thought it would be our oldest son who was destined. But Amatus told us no. From then on, he said no to the next four children, but when he saw you,

He joyfully proclaimed you as the one promised. Head Bishop Amatus is a man you can trust. He sees many visions from the Master. He saw your birth and some future days of yours. Now, he didn't impart much to us, but he did say you were to be great.

A leader who would bring many to the master. But he also saw what would happen if you were to choose the dark path of the soul snatcher. Chaos will reign, Light Followers will perish, and the entire teachings of the academy will die and be forgotten.

I give you a good warning, my son. Guard yourself. Be careful. The Soul Snatcher is crafty and will try all of his ways of darkness to turn you onto his side and use you for destruction.

# The Letter

AGE is an amazing school. Learn all you can and gather around you trustworthy, loyal friends who also walk in the light. Good luck, my son. Follow the Master and be faithful to all His teachings."

Your Father,

Bartimus

P.S. Be wary of the Swamps of Hatred. Many students have been hypnotized into giving away their souls. Farewell, my son. Alexander shivered as he stared at the letter, trying to comprehend what he had just read. He reread it. Still confused, he reread it once more.

"Alex, is that you?" Beck asked Blurrily, rubbing his eyes. But when he opened them once again, the room was dark, and not a sound could be heard. Alexander waited tensely until Beck laid back down, and he could hear the even rhythm of his breathing. He silently folded the letter, stuffed it back under his pillow, and lay down, attempting to get at least a little bit of sleep in the midst of the thoughts circling around in his head.

*****************************************

"Okay, class, listen up." The headmaster and Dr. Skane stood in front of Mrs. Good's classroom, addressing the students. "Mrs. Good has come down with a cold and is unable to teach, so Dr. Skane will be filling in until such a time she is able to return. Please listen to him and be as attentive as you would if she were present." He looked at the class troublemakers briefly, then turned on his heel and walked out the door.

The children all looked around at each other in glee. Snippets could be heard filtering throughout the class: "I'm so glad she's gone," "Yes, no more rules," "Relaxation time." The last comment came directly from Beck, who immediately, upon the departure of Headmaster Carethemost, slouched at his desk.

"Now, children," Dr. Skane addressed them disapprovingly, "Mrs. Good is a fine teacher, and we all hope she will return to good health quickly. So, I will hear no more chortling and rejoicing about her absence." He gave the class a hard stare and held it a little longer on Beck, who quickly straightened his desk and attempted to look innocent. "Good, that's settled then," Dr. Skane continued. "Today, we will learn about covetousness and discontentment. I would like for each of you to pair up and see what you can find.".

The students sprang into action as he dismissed them to start their research. They all chose their partners quickly and efficiently. Tara stared into space while Beck and Xander elevatored away to level Sudoxe after studying the level cheat sheet.

Olivia approached Lucy. "Will you study with me?" she inquired. Lucy looked over at Tara and waited a minute, trying to get Tara to look at her.

Tara ignored her and continued staring at the front of the classroom, deep in her own thoughts. Lucy turned back to Olivia and gave her a small smile. "Sure, I'll go with you, thanks." She looked over her shoulder at Tara as she and Olivia walked toward the table. Tara made no change in her concentration. Lucy shook her head and tried to look happy, but inside, she was confused and sad that Tara did not seem to care about the fact that they were separate.

✻✻✻✻✻✻✻✻✻✻✻✻✻✻✻✻

"So, what did the letter say?" Beck pulled on Alexander's sleeve and urged an answer out of his friend as soon as they were remotely alone.

Alexander turned and pulled the letter out of his trouser pocket. "Here, read it for yourself. See what you think.".

Beck took the letter gleefully and skimmed its single page. The more he read, the more he looked confused. He reread the letter again, reading a bit slower. After reading it several times, he looked at Xander with a very perplexed face and asked, "Is it true the Head Bishop prophesied your birth? You're going to be a great leader some day."

Xander shrugged his shoulders and pocketed the letter once more. "See, I don't know; that's why I have to go see the Headmaster and see if he will let me go see Bishop Amatus." Alexander suddenly sobbed his face and struck a pose as he pointed to Beck, "What doest thou in the Great Leader Presence? Kneel Peasant!" Beck's eyes went wide in shock as he stared at Xander. Alexander laughed at Beck's stupefied face. "I'm joking! So, what if someone thinks I'm going to be a great leader? I don't care.".

Beck returned to his normal smiling self once he recovered from his friend's sudden outburst. "Just wait till this gets out. If it's true, you will be famous, and I'm your best friend, so I'll be  famous!" He laughed heartily, very happy with that prospect.

Xander was rueful. "Yeah, sure," he said. "Famous and marked."

The boys monkeyed around, finding ancient stories of discontentment and of children suffering in a desert for a long time. They discussed the different topics they could choose from. Xander noticed Beck was getting quieter and quieter.

Finally, Beck had enough. "Okay, I'll say it." He raised his hands in resignation.

Xander looked at him, confused. "Say what?"

Beck looked irked as he stared at the floor for a moment. "I'm just boring." He finally said, "I have no cool prophecies about me, so I'm just lame.".

Alexander smiled, then burst out laughing, "You are not lame; you're normal, and that's better than anything else. Plus, I wasn't even thinking about that."

"Oh well, me neither; I wasn't thinking about it either," Beck mumbled as he kicked a small pebble that bounced off the toe of his shoe. He looked over at Xander, who was still looking at him with a comical expression on his face, and they both busted out laughing over Beck's momentary pouting jealously.

"What are you two so merry about?" Tara's sharp voice sobbed them up quickly.

Beck was the first to recover. "Ugh, what do you care, you stuffed-up turkey buzzard?" He retorted. He received a wack on the arm for his efforts.

"All I know is that this institution lacks reading materials; I wish I had more books to study, and I especially wish you two weren't always in my way!" She turned on her heel and stomped away in a huff.

Beck whistled low and quiet as she walked away. "Man, what happened to her? She ruined her favorite pair of stockings, or what?"

"I don't know," Xander replied, watching Tara walk away. "But we better keep an eye on her. She's bound to trip with her knickers that twisted." And with that, they cackled down the main hall.

As the students were released for lunch, Alexander spotted Mr. Carethemost in his office. He walked over and knocked on the door frame.

Carethmost looked up from a book he had in his hand, and his face broke into a smile. "Ah, Alexander. Do come in. How is your first term going?" He jokingly greeted Xander and patted the seat next to him, inviting the young lad to take a seat.

Xander sat down beside him and fidgeted nervously. "It's going well, sir."

Carethemost, who could very easily tell the boy had something on his mind due to all the nervous twitching, set his book down and gave Xander his full attention. "Good, what can I do for you, young man?"

# The Letter

"Well, sir," Alexander paused for a moment and then reached into his trousers and pulled out the letter. He just held it, looking at it in his lap for a minute.

Carethemost smiled, "Ah yes, the letter. Quite a shock. I'm sure you must have a lot of questions." Xander nodded but just sat there, still trying to come up with a good way to present his request to see Head Bishop Amatus.

Before he could form any words, Carethemost saved him the trouble. He said jokingly, "Well, I think it would be best if Mr. Amatus explained it. Come. Step lively now onto the elevator platform." Carethmost made sure Xander was secured with his seatbelt. "Now, son, when you are ready, Trace out HBS. Once you arrive, you will see twelve doors. Go to the one that is unmarked. All the others will have symbols, but find the unmarked door quickly because the symbols will change doors, and you will have to find the bare door again. Do you understand?"

Xander nodded as Carethmost came to stand next to him and whispered in his ear, "The password is J twenty-nine colon eleven. There should be a keypad there; just type it in, and the door will swing open on its own."

Barely before Alexander could nod in acknowledgment, he disappeared from sight, gliding until he came to a stop in a bare, empty room with one light extended from the ceiling. Surrounding him were the twelve doors Carethemost had told him about. The room was a perfect circle. No signs or pictures were hung on the walls between the twelve doors. He quickly surveyed each door, and once he found the one with no symbol, he ran to it and typed in the code before the doors could switch.

Upon typing in the directed password, The door instantly swung open, and before Xander sat a huge wooden statue of an eagle. He stood there in awe, staring at the intricate carving, his mouth slightly agape.

"Magnificent creatures, aren't they?" Startled, Alexander turned toward the voice to see an old man sitting in a chair by a crackling fire. The man smiled at Alexander and said, "I apologize. I did not mean to frighten you. You must be Alexander." He motioned for Xander to come sit in the chair opposite him.

Xander walked over towards the older man. He looked around at his surroundings, taking everything in. The office he walked through was magnificent. Large, two-story windows with long, flowing curtains were on all sides of them. His desk sat in the center, covered in half-written notes, orders, and sermons. In the corner where they now sat were two plush leather chairs and the crackling warmth of the fireplace. Above them, on the mantle, a beautiful sword with a long, shiny blade hung beside a full set of silver armor.

Wide-eyed Alexander looked back at Amatus, or so he hoped, for he had never before seen the man and was not sure what to expect.

Amatus in turn, gazed at the young man before him—more boy than man, it seemed, for he looked very young with a slight build and mischievous brown eyes and hair that looked like it did not want to be controlled. But the boy displayed a confidence that he didn't always feel.

Amatus finally broke the silence. "I see the letter has reached you." He looked down at the letter Xander was still holding in his hand.

Xander swallowed and nodded. "Yes, sir, it did."

"And do you have questions for me?" Xander nodded once again at Amatus' inquiry. Amatus smiled and said softly, "I am guessing you would like the whole story?" Alexander once again nodded without saying anything.

The head bishop sat back in his chair and began his story.

# Chapter 9
# The Boy of Promise

Amatus made his way through the blowing sand. He looked up as his scarf wrapped around his face to see his guide steadily trudging his way up yet another mountain of sand. It was the coldest part of the year, and Amatus was exceedingly grateful, as he could not imagine the heat this wretched desert could produce.

Months earlier, he would have never imagined being here. He considered how it came to be, for there he was in his study with the other members. Hashing out plans for a new institution, The men were also considering how to process the large amounts of books and manuscripts that would be needed.

The plan they were discussing was an academy where children could go to study the true holy arts without confusion with the larger world. A place where children and youth alike could be young and free without being endangered. These children would grow up and embrace the master's teaching and follow his path while being taught to avoid the dark works of the soul snatcher.

But as the men sat arguing the details about acquiring land, teachers, offices, room and board, Apothecary, and so much more, a boy arrived with the Daily Post. Amatus gave him the money needed for the daily post, then sat back to read while the men argued in the background. He scanned the headlines. The depression seemed to be engulfing the entire world. Suddenly, an article of a man in front of a large temple covered in stone situated in the middle of the desert caught his eye. He quickly scanned the article, grasping the main parts of the story.

'Huge Temple Discovered'

'Impossible to Open'

'If opened, it is to be believed there is a sphinx inside that prophesies.'

# The Boy of Promise

'Come one, come all to answer the great door riddle.'

Amatus left off reading, "Gentlemen!" The men all stopped and turned to look at him. "I'm going to Africa." He placed the paper on the table calmly in front of him as if this were a daily announcement he made: "If I am successful, I will ask the Sphynx what we should do about our ideas here today and who should lead us."

Now thousands of miles away, Amatus doubted his wisdom in rushing into the middle of the desert with its endless sand and with only one man whom he had just met, who, for a price, had agreed to take him to the temple.

Another hour slides by. Amatus starts to feel his age. He begins to imagine how good it would feel to be sitting by the fire enjoying a cup of his newest coffee roast as his favorite record, 'Fur Elise,' played softly in the background.

His guide suddenly stopped and pointed, quivering at the massive fourteen-story structure with surrounding walls in the distance. Turrets on every corner and the peaks of many buildings could be seen over the twenty-foot walls.

A man approached the large front door. A voice speaks to him too far away for Amatus to hear. Amatus watches as the man contemplates for a moment, then assuredly answers. "WRONG!" A voice bellows. The ground shook and trembled, and the man cried out as he fell through the whole that opened in the earth below him. As quickly as everything started, it came to a stop. Not even dust swirled around. Everything was eerily silent.

Amatus stood there in silence. The shock was pounding through his body as he tried to wrap his mind around what had just happened. He looked over to see where his guide was. No one was there. He turned around to see his guide running as fast as he could, tripping and falling several times as he tried to outrun his own legs.

Amatus took a deep breath, and with steely resolve and a prayer sent up to the master, he cautiously approached the temple gate.

As he stood there, looking up at the ancient stone gate, a low, growling voice greeted him.

'I was never born.'

'I Have No End'

'I am inevitable'

'But I cannot be seen.'

'What Am I?'

Amatus slowly rolled the riddle around in his head. He was worried now. Back in the council room, he considered himself a fairly wise man, but here, all alone, he wondered if that were true. After considering it for a while longer, he took a breath and said, "You are Eternity!" The long silence that followed his answer had Amatus worried, and he started slowly moving away from the door of the temple.

Then, to his surprise, the gate crumbled to dust. A large archway gaped at him, seemingly to beckon him forward. Amatus entered the courtyard. All the buildings surrounding him were empty. He could see large steps leading upward, but before he could begin to climb them, the temple shook, and the Sphinx rose from the sand in front of him.

"What would you ask of me?" The Sphinx's voice had a gravelly death note sound to it: "You may ask me two questions. Choose them wisely.".

Amatus shuddered at the deadly voice. "I would ask you to tell me my future."

"I know your desires!" The Sphynx's shouting echoed through the desert: "But let me warn you, nothing good comes from learning about your future!"

Amatus nodded. "I accept my fate.".

"Very well, you shall succeed with your academy, and you shall lead, but there will come a child greater than you to either destroy your school or preserve it."

"How will I know him?" Amatus inquired.

The Sphynx replied, "He will come from a complicated family; he will have a birthmark on his face!"

Slowly, the sphynx melted back into the sand. The temple started shaking. Then, it crumbled and completely disappeared. Amatus was left alone in the vast desert.

"But how did you get home?" Alexander brought Amatus out of his reverie.

Amatus smiled. "Oh, I wandered for a stretch, and then some camel merchants came along and helped me to the nearest city."

"So I am really going to lead?" Alexander asked timidly.

Amatus put his hand on Xander's shoulder tenderly and said, "Yes, my son, your time will come. But for now, study hard and don't worry about it. Prepare yourself for the time that approaches, and you would do well to be prepared."

Alexander wandered aimlessly through the halls after leaving Head Bishop Amatus' office. In his shocked reverie, he walked right past Beck, who hollered his name, "Xander! There you are. Where'd you go?"

Alexander turned towards him, still a bit dazed, and said, "I came from Mr. Amatus' office.".

"Did he tell you anything?" Beck asked, seemingly not noticing the strange look on Xander's face.

Xander nodded slowly. "I was prophesied by a Sphynx.".

"A Sphynx? Jingle bells!" Beck exploded at that: "You know, I don't think I want to hear anymore. All I got was my old Granny, who told my mom, 'Ruby looks like you're going to have another one,' and mom was already 6 months pregnant. No, DUH Granny".

Alexander laughed and said, "Come on, let's find Lucy and Tara, and I'll tell them and you the whole story.

Upon finding the girls, Xander did his best to explain to all his friends what the letter had said as well as the story Head Bishop Amatus had told him. In the end, he sat looking around at his friends, worried they would think him odd for the prophecy.

Lucy spoke up first: "Wow! So you're like royalty or something.".

Xander shrugged. "I guess sort of, but please don't tell anyone, guys." He looked from Lucy to Beck.

Beck groaned, "But I already told like ten people in my head that I was going to make us famous."

Lucy and Xander laughed at poor Beck. Then Lucy whispered, "I have news as well." The boys leaned in close. "I was walking by the infirmary when I heard Nurse Nancy speaking to the Head Master." She paused and glanced around to assure their privacy before she continued, "Nurse Nancy was showing Mr. Carethemost an empty container. I don't know what it was, but she said she never used it because it was poisonous and could hurt someone in large doses. She did say there were supposed to be ten vials in the container. The Head Master acted very calm and assured her they were probably misplaced, but when he left, he looked very concerned indeed."

Beck looked at Alexander worriedly. "Who would need to poison someone?"

Alexander and Lucy spoke in unison, "Dr. Skane."

"Yes, what can I do for you?" The children jumped as the voice spoke from behind them. They turned to see Dr. Skane standing there, smiling at them with his hands clasped behind his back.

# Chapter 10
# Suspicions

The children stood, looking up at the man they were just speaking about. "Well?" Dr. Skane raised his eyebrows, waiting for the answer from the three.

"We, uh, we were just wondering," Lucy trailed off as Alexander jumped in.

"If you enjoyed teaching our class," He finished.

Dr. Skane smiled and said, "Oh, I quite enjoy it, especially with children as special as you." As he said this, he looked directly at Xander. Xander squirmed and looked away, afraid his face would show too much. Dr. Skane then nodded to them all and told them to have a good day as he continued walking toward his room, leaving the children conflicted.

Beck broke the silence. "Did you see that look he gave you?" He looked at Xander, who was watching the door Dr. Skane had just entered.

"I know, but maybe he just knows the prophecy or something. I'm not sure." Xander replied, finally looking at his friends. He shrugged as he said, "Come on. Let's go."

As the children sat in the grand hall at breakfast the next morning, Lucy, Xander, and Beck brought Tara up to speed on all the recent happenings she had missed.

Tara looked skeptical the entire time they spoke. Once they finished their story and they all sat back, she scowled as she said to Xander, "A skinny, timid boy like you... A Leader? Rubbish. And is Dr. Skane a poisoner? Literally, you guys don't have enough to do, apparently." She huffed as she started eating her breakfast.

"See, I told you we shouldn't have told her," Beck muttered to Alexander as he picked slowly at his food.

Xander elbowed Beck and looked at Tara. "Look. You don't have to believe us or go with us, but we need your help getting into Dr. Skane's room."

"Forget it, Alex. She'll never help us." Beck waved a resigned hand toward Tara.

Tara glared at Beck, who promptly pretended he was eating busily. "I will help merely to spite you." She jabbed a finger toward Beck and said, "But I'm only going to say, 'I told you so' when we don't find anything."

Beck pointed back at Tara mockingly, "We don't need your help; we'll just pop the window, sneak in and explore the room, and sneak back out. Simple." Beck smiled triumphantly at Lucy and Xander as he stood up to leave.

Lucy reached up, grabbed Beck's shirt, and pulled him back down to his seat. "No, it's not going to be that easy.".

"Lucy is right," Alexander agreed. "We are going to have to do it during class; otherwise, Skane might walk in on us." Xander looked over to Beck and said, "And we can't sneak in through the window because they have shutters that lock on the inside, and I am pretty sure all the teachers keep them closed and locked. So we will have to go through the teacher's dorm without being seen and enter Skanes room. Look for our evidence and get out before any of the teachers see us."

Tara made a small face. "And what if the door to Dr. Skanes's room is locked?"

Alexander looked thoughtfully into space for a minute. "I got it! In the next few weeks, Beck and I will volunteer to clean the teacher's dorm, and we'll check out the layout and see if the teachers lock their room doors. In the meantime, you girls decide what time would be best and try to plan where the teachers would probably be." He stopped and looked around at all his friends, who looked a bit skeptical of his plan. "Got it?"

Beck frowned. "Yeah, we got it. I don't know why I have to do the cleaning."

"You got a better plan?" Xander asked. Beck mumbled and shook his head. "Okay, then. That's the plan." Xander stood as the bell rang for classes, which took them away from their plans.

**************************

"He knows," The eleven council members looked at Amatus as he spoke, "The boys know who he is now. The time is near."

One Minister rose to his feet, "What should we do to prepare?"

Amatus motioned him to sit back down, "Nothing. He is safe here but I do feel as if we should all visit the Academy frequently and increase our effort to keep dark communication from the school. Also, we will have to be on the lookout for any signed that the Soul Snatcher has located him. I have a dark feeling I cannot shake that someone is not who they say they are."

****************************

"Alright, Class, Your study period starts now." Dr. Skane stood at the front of the classroom; he was still substituting. He dismissed them and settled into his chair to read.

The students begin taking turns on the elevator. Alexander, Lucy, Beck, and Tara were elevated to the first floor of Siseneg and snuck into chapter room 27.

"Did you girls figure it out?" Alexander whispered from where he stood by the doorway, watching for other students.

"The best time that we can figure out is when we all go to play Begotten. The teachers all go to the Grand Hall for lunch, and of course, everyone else besides the nurses is on the field engaged in the game. And the nurses probably won't see us if we are super quiet." Tara whispered back.

"Excellent!" Xander exclaimed and then immediately lowered his voice as he remembered what they were discussing: "But we can't all go then because our team would be four short, and others would be sure to notice if we were all missing. So we will draw straws to see which two of us will go and which two will play." They all agreed to the plan.

Xander continued, "Okay, so for Beck and me, as we cleaned the teacher's dorms last week, we noticed that only Dr. Skane and Mr. Shy locked their doors. We tried to peek in through the peep hole, but to no avail."

"Did you get to see where he hid the key?" Lucy asked.

Beck groaned, "Yes, we've seen where he puts it." Beck slumped against the wall with a defeated look on his face. "It's impossible to get to.".

"Is that true?" Tara looked at Alexander, who looked downcast as well.

"Yes, it's true. He gives it to a pigeon, who flies away until evening. We tried to follow it once, but it always goes into the swamp of hatred and never comes back until he calls it back when he needs the key."

Lucy's face suddenly brightened with an idea: "Could we duplicate it?"

Xander looked at her, then slowly started smiling with a mischievous glint in his eye. He turned to Tara and asked, "Do you remember that hardening gunk you told me to use for my torn-up shoes?" Tara nodded, trying to figure out what the shoe gunk had to do with their predicament. "Where could we get some?" Xander asked.

"Well, we could try the merchant seller that comes by once a month. Or maybe one of the other students brought some from home." Tara shrugged.

Xander grinned. "Okay, guys, spread out. We gotta find some."

"But, Xander, what will we do with it?" Lucy grabbed his arm before he could dart off to start looking.

"If we find some, Beck and I can squeeze it into the key hole. Put a stick in, and then when it hardens, it should act as a key. Therefore, unlocking the door." Xander looked like he had just solved the biggest mystery ever.

Tara folded her arms defiantly. "And what makes you think that it will be you and Beck that will be the ones to do it?"

"Ugh, Tara, whatever. Whoever goes will unlock the door. Great?" Alex glanced at them and said, "Great!".

As Xander and Beck walked off to start their search for shoes, Beck mumbled, "It will be us that go, right?"

Xander grinned wickedly. "Oh yes, most definitely." The boys cackled as they continued down the hall.

After their study period was over, Beck approached Drew. He was at his wit's end. He had been all over every dorm. He had even approached Marstin but had no luck. No one had any shoe gunk for the key hole.

Alexander and Lucy were following Dr. Skane around, trying to choreograph and memorize his movements throughout the day after their class. And Tara, as always, was studying for a test.

'Pff,' Beck thought, 'She is always studying.' He mused about the way her toes dipped in when she was concentrating and how her... Beck slapped himself. "Yuck, gross, she's a girl," he mumbled. "Even worse, she's Tara. But he couldn't help thinking a little more about the girl who troubled him so much: 'She's charming and kind of cute when she doesn't know he can see her. "Ugh, no, no." He slapped himself again. He was a man going on thirteen; he needed to find Drew and ask about Shoe Goo. He had more important things to do. He didn't need to do any more thinking. Thinking is bad.

Meanwhile, as Beck was arguing with his inner thoughts, Alexander dove behind a stone pillar at the front of the academy, pulling Lucy behind him. They had been watching Skane for an hour, but he hadn't moved much. At the moment, he sat under a tree, chomping on an apple and enjoying a book.

Alexander motioned for Lucy, "Let's go. We won't learn anything here at this rate."

Dr. Skane heard a rustle in the bushes to his left. Looking up, he saw two bodies disappearing around the corner of the Main Academy building. A smile tugged at his lips as he went back to his book.

Beck found Drew and Jonathan knee-deep in a game of Viking Chess. "Who's winning?" He asked, walking up to their table.

"Oh, we are actually pretty even right now," Jonathan replied without taking his eyes off the board in front of him.

"Cool, cool," Beck tried to act casual. "Say, Drew, would you happen to have any of that gunk that fixes shoes?"

"Yep, sure do. What will you give me for it?" Drew moved one of his chess pieces as he talked.

Beck dug into his pockets and said, "I got a Deutsche mark I found in the dirt.".

Drew looked up from his game; his attention was finally captured. "Let's see it." The boys leaned in close as Beck flashed the coin at them. Flipping it in the air and catching it again. Holding it up between his fingers, he produced it closer to Drew.

"Sooo, whatcha think?" He looked at Drew expectantly, who immediately dashed to his bed and pulled out his trunk from underneath it. He returned to Drew with the shoe goo in his hand, and the boys exchanged treasures.

Beck left the boys with a "Good luck on the game." Tossing over his shoulder, he ran to go find Alex. As he tore around the corner of the dorm, he ran right into Dr. Skane.

Dr. Skane toppled and grabbed Beck's shoulder to steady himself. "Whooaa, son, Whats the rush?" He held Beck with one big hand and peered at him discerningly.

Beck's eyes widened in shock. "I'm sorry, sir; I was just running to go find Xander." Beck stammered as he held the glue in a tight grip behind his back.

Dr. Skanes eyes narrowed. "Well, is he on death row or something? Slow down. You could hurt someone." He released Beck's shoulder and straightened the uniform he had wrinkled.

Beck nodded quickly. "Yeah, si, I'm sorry, sir."

Dr. Skane smiled and said, "No, not to worry. What do you have behind your back?" He asked knowingly.

Beck glanced down, bringing his hands forward. "It's really nothing, sir, just some shoe glue, sir." He held the shoe goo up for inspection.

Dr. Skanes dark brows rose. "Shoe glue, eh? Well, carry on, then. Just slow  down." He stepped out of the way, allowing Beck to pass. Beck's heart shuddered against his ribs as he half-walked and half-ran for the Main Hall.

Alexander and Lucy found Tara hiding in the small library on the main floor. It was off the main hall, right after Mr. Shy's classroom. As the door opened, Tara glanced up and asked, "What do you want?" She marked her spot in the book and laid it on the nearby class table.

Xander flopped down on a nearby chair and said, "If Beck finds the glue, I think we can go tomorrow. So we need to choose who is going." Just as he finished speaking, Beck burst through the door.

"I think he knows," Beck panted, putting his hands on his knees as he tried to catch his breath.

"Who knows what?" Xander sat up and raised his eyebrows toward his exhausted friend.

"Dr. Skane, I ran into him, and he saw the glue gunk." Beck was still panting and wheezing out.

"How could he possibly deduce that we're?" Tara lowered her voice. "Trying to sneak into his bedroom?"

Beck shrugged. "He knows. I just know he knows. Even if he doesn't know he knows, I know he knows," Beck nodded affirmatively at his reasoning.

Lucy glanced around at each of them and asked, "So, should we still go through with it?"

Xander stood and walked over toward Beck. "I'm going, and Beck is coming with me." He placed a hand on Beck's shoulder.

"Who?! Me?!" asked Beck, very alarmed by the sudden decision. He looked at Xander like Xander had two heads. "Did you not just hear me? He's on to us. He KNOWS".

Xander grinned at him, then soberingly said, "Look, if Dr. Skane did poison Mrs. Good so he could get closer to me, and if he knows who I am and is thinking of harming me or anyone else, I'd kind of like to know. So I am going, whether one of you comes with me or not."

The other three looked at Alexander, surprised. He never got so riled up before. "Wow, maybe you are going to be a leader someday," Tarah complimented. "Okay, then you and Beck go, and me and Lucy will be your lookouts. If any teachers head that way, we will let you know somehow."

Xander nodded. "Okay, that sounds good. We will go tomorrow." He started at the library door.

Beck ran up to walk with him. "When you said me, you really meant Lucy, right?" Alex laughed at Beck's concerned face and walked out the door, towing a reluctant Beck behind him.

******************************

"So no one will need to turn in their papers tomorrow. Class is dismissed." Dr. Skane released the class and started tidying his desk as the students bolted for the door. "Walk, children. Please walk," he hollered towards them.

Then, returning his gaze towards his desk, he noticed Tara sitting at her desk, still reading attentively. "Tara," he called out, "you're dismissed." He motioned toward the door.

Tara closed her book quickly. "Oh, sorry, Dr. Skane. I just wanted to finish my chapter before recess. And now I have. Thank you, Dr. Skane."

Dr. Skane shook his head and said, "Yes, yes, now go have fun." He wiggled his fingers at her and said, "Leave your books. My word, child, you study too much. Sometimes you just need to let go and have a little play time."

Tara nodded and blushed a bit. "Yes, sir, I'll just return this book to the library and then go out for recess."

"There's a good girl, Tata." Wiggling his fingers at her in a dismissive motion, he settled back into his chair.

Standing at the door that opened towards the field, Alexander, Beck, and Lucy stood huddled together and asked, "Where is Tara?" Alexander whispered toward Lucy.

Lucy shrugged. "I don't know. She was supposed to follow me out."

Xander glanced around and said, "Well, just go out and play. Me and Beck will go ahead with the plan." Beck and Alex waited in the bathroom until silence rang in the halls. Quietly, they tiptoed out the double doors on the right side of the academy, away from the game and the other students, whose laughter and squeals could be heard all around the court. Slowly, they silently made their way toward the teacher's dorms.

Meanwhile, Tara opened the library door. The lights were off, so it was fairly dim, but she didn't mind, as she knew this room by heart, and the open door shed enough light that she could see the shelves faintly. She confidently walked to the third row of bookshelves. Suddenly, the door creaked to a close, blotting out all light.

*************************************

Henry looked around amidst the running students, finding Lucy he ran over and leaned down so he could talk quietly, "Alexander and Beck wouldn't be doing something they shouldn't be, would they?"

Lucy looked agitated at his question, "Well… um well…" She didn't finish. She could tell by the look on Henry's face that he was already thinking they were up to no good.

"Come, Lucy, we're going to the Head Master."

**************************************

Alexander and Beck softly entered the teacher's dorm. Quietly, they crept to Dr Skanes bedroom door. Alexander took the shoe glue out of his pocket and began squirting it into the key hole. Sticking the stick into it quickly while it hardened so they had a handle.

Beck shifted from one foot to the other, nervously glancing around, "Hurry, Xander." He urged.

"I'm trying to. It's a small keyhole, you know. I have to hold this stick here until it hardens, you know".

****************************************

Tara swung around; alarmed, she slowly backed against the wall.

"Tara," A slimy, slick voice rasped her name.

Tara opened her mouth to scream but no sound game escaped her lips. She pushed herself as close to the wall as she good, feeling the shelf behind her dig into her back.

Two yellow eyes stared deep into her Soul. They seemed to be moving closer to her slowly, almost as if stalking her, "Come, Tara, Come with me," The voice rasped, definitely closer than it was before, "I have a special job for you."

****************************************

"Henry, noooo!" Lucy jerked on Henry's hand that had her by the wrist as he drug her towards the Main Hall.

"It's for Alexanders good. I don't want him to get hurt." Henry stopped pulling her. "Look, Lucy, I'm sorry, but I'm not about to lose Begotten and have to sing on my last year here, okay. So let's find Alexander and Beck so we can start playing, alright?".

******************************************

Tara felt as if she was in a dream as her legs carried her to the table in the middle of the library. She felt herself being transported in a daze down a row and to the right. She opened the door to the council room and walked forward. No one was in sight as she looked at all the volumes of books stretching from top to bottom.

"Place it on the shelf marked 'most safe.'" The deathly voice moved her. She took the book that had somehow appeared into her hands and moved towards the shelf that was indicated. Reaching the shelf, she slid the book into place. The voice cackled in a low, evil tone, "Good, good."

*****************************************

"Okay, It's dry. Time to see if it worked," Alexander slowly turned the hardened glue, and slowly, the lock turned and clicked. Slowly, the door inched open. Xander peaked inside and then threw the door wide open. There was nothing. Absolutely nothing. Just four bone bare walls and an empty floor.

Beck Peeked around the corner cautiously, and his eyes widened, "Jiminie, What does he sleep on?" Beck and Xander stared dumbfounded.

"In my bed." A voice behind them spoke. Alexander and Beck jumped as if they were shot. They slowly turned around to face a very unhappy HeadMaster, Carethemost, Dr Skane, Henry, and Lucy.

# Chapter 11
# Punishment

Tara woke suddenly, jerking awake. She was sitting at the library with a book of insects in her hands. She blinked, confused. She had never fallen asleep while reading before. Quickly, she ran into the main hall just in time to see Alexander, Lucy, Beck, Henry, Dr. Skane, and the Headmaster walk into Carethemost's office. She called out to them, but Dr. Skane shut and barred the door before anyone noticed her.

Carethemost sat down in his chair, looking at Henry. He said, "You may go, Henry. I will take it from here, but you will hear from me about not keeping your dorm boys in line." Henry nodded silently and exited the room.

Turning to an ashamed Beck and Xander, he said, "Did Lucy help you in any way get into Dr. Skanes's room?"

Alexander looked up quickly and said, "No, sir. It was all my doing." Carethemost assessed Xander for a moment as if trying to discern if he was telling the truth. Then he looked at Lucy and said, "Very well, Miss Lucy. You are free to go."

A slight rap on the door interrupted them. Dr. Skane walked in and opened the door. Before him stood Head Bishop Amatus. "May I come in?" Amatus asked politely.

"Absolutely, Amatus, come in," Carethemost waved him in, and the old friends shook hands.

Amatus looked around at the tense room and the two boys, who looked like they were about to be sentenced to death. "Don't mind me. Carry on. I am just a bystander. Do as you deem fit; I am aware of the grievance that was  committed." Amatus stepped off to the side and observed silently.

Carethemost turned his attention to the two remaining boys and said, "I am not interested in why you did what you did, but I am disappointed you broke the rules, and I am even more grieved that you left your teammates to go monkeyshine, and now your dorm has to suffer the consequences with you as they lost another chance to win. I want you both to consider how you neglected to think of your friends."

"Furthermore," he continued, "as for punishment, I believe I will leave it to Dr. Skane's capable hands." Carethemost beckoned Dr. Skane to speak.

Dr. Skane considered the boys for a moment, then, coming to a conclusion, he finally spoke, "Well, I believe a late-night maze run would suffice." He looked for contradictions. Seeing none, he continued, "If you would be kind enough to refresh my memory on how it works and help me design a suitable maze for this occasion," He looked at the headmaster.

Carethemost nodded. "Of course, straightaway. You boys are confined to your rooms for the rest of the day."

Carethemost stopped at Amatus' raised hand and said, "If I might have a word with the boys, I will make sure to escort them to their dorm." Amatus walked closer.

"As you wish, Amatus." Carethmost and Skane proceeded outside on their way to the maze.

Amatus turned towards the boys and said, "As for what Mr. Carethmost said, I, on the other hand, would very much like to know the reason for your disobedience to the rules."

The boys looked at each other, deliberating if they wanted to spill their secrets. Then, with a small nod to each other, they launched into the whole story, often speaking over each other in their hurry to explain all their reasoning to Amatus, who listened attentively to each and every detail. Once the boys were finished, they waited in breathless silence as Amatus sat for a moment, staring at them deep in thought.

Finally, he spoke, "And after everything, did you find anything to prove your belief?"

"No, not a thing," Beck responded quietly. "The room was empty.".

Amatus smiled thoughtfully. "Well, I suggest you look elsewhere then. Not that I condone what you boys did today. Also, I hope you don't try sneaking into my room next." He chuckled, lightening the somber mood. "Now shoo to your rooms, no dedawdlin." He stood and walked to the door, prompting them to make their way.

As they walked past the door, saying their goodbyes to Amatus, Tara was waiting for them on the outside of the door. "Oh, now you show up," Beck spat at her, looking betrayed.

"I didn't mean to... I…" Tara frowned and looked down as she looked like she was trying to remember something. "Never mind. I hate you, Beck." She ran out of the building toward her room.

"What a crybaby; she plays around while we get in trouble." Beck shook his head as he glared toward Tara's retreating form.

Xander lightly punched his shoulder. "Chill out, Beck; I'm sure she had a good reason. I'm not sure what, but we knew the risk we were taking." They passed other students as they made their way to their dorm. The looks of anger and malice came from their teammates.

Marstin gaffawed and heckled them as he passed. "Well, well, look who it is—the boys who got lost in their game of playing dollies and couldn't make it to an actual game."

Alexander and Beck did their best to ignore the big bully and push through the gathering of students who were standing by the exit door closest to their dorm. Once they were safely through the throng and the door to their room was shut tightly, Alexander excitedly pulled something from his pocket, holding it in front of Beck with a look of triumph on his face.

"What? It's a feather."

"Exactly! A pigeon feather said, "Come," an Alex pulled Beck to the right-side window facing their playground for Begotten. "See, right there is where they keep the carrier pigeons for when they need to send messages to the other academies or to anyone else, really. But the point is, How did this feather get to the other side of the academy and into Dr. Skanes's room?"

"Uh, wind, maybe," Beck looked unconvinced. His eyebrows quirked in a way that seemed to say, 'I don't care. I've had enough trouble for one day.'

Xander rolled his eyes and said, "No, you fruitloop, not wind."

"Then what?"

"I don't know, but I will find out." Alexander began to muse, twirling the pigeon feather between his forefinger and thumb. Beck started worrying about their punishment. He hated the maze, especially in the dark.

At dusk, they followed Dr. Skane and Headmaster Carethemost to the maze, dreading every step they took that took them closer to the looming hedges.

Carethemost stopped by the maze. The six-foot shrub brushes had been aligned accordingly. Dr. Skane had drawn an impressively huge twisting and turning maze with the entrance and exit side by side. Looking closer at the walls, the boys could see they wouldn't be able to just crouch low and fight their way through the wall, as either side was a solid mesh of large poisonous thorns.

"Here's an oil lamp for you." Carethemost handed Xander a small lamp with a red handle and said, "And don't worry, we teachers will spell each other off, waiting for you to get out. So someone will always be within shouting distance."

"But what if we can't find our way out?" Xander asked, looking a bit frightened at the thought.

"If in the morning you are still lost, we can simply look at the white board and know exactly where you are located, and we will come find you. But before you go, I believe apologies are in order." Carethemost turned to where Dr. Skane was watching him instruct the boys.

Alexander and Beck both turned to Dr. Skane and said simultaneously, "We truly are very sorry, sir. It won't happen again."

"I accept your apology and forgive you." Dr. Skane gave them each a small kiss and a pat on the shoulder. "Now, good luck to you both."

The boys slowly walked into the towering shrubs. As they made their second tern, Beck's mouth came alive. "Good luck!" Good Luck?! Pttsh, what does he care?" He changed his voice so he was speaking through his nose: "'Now don't ever do it again. Here's an oil lamp.' Doesn't he know this thing is as worthless as closing your eyes and trying to read?"

Alexander ignored his friends, ranting. Determination coursed through him as he tried to make heads or tails of where they were. On and on, they walked. Beck's whining never ceased to the point Alexander started to pray Beck's tongue would just fall out of his mouth."

After two hours of turnarounds and dead ends, no answer to his previous prayer, and no worthwhile help from a grumbling Beck, he was about to give up. He had already given up the hope of Beck ever shutting up. But he just knew if he could get to the center, he had an idea that might get them out of here before daylight.

******************************

"Where were you?" Lucy and Tara sat in silence, glaring at each other, sparks flying from their eyes.

"I don't know. Its all hazy, and I don't remember. I feel like I was maybe dreaming, but I don't think I fell asleep."

Lucy huffed, "You are your obsession with knowing everything is going to kill someone one day."

# Punishment

"Oh, Oh, my bad! Maybe I should be like brainless Beck or prophecied Xander". Tara looked away, but Lucy saw what looked like tears in her eyes.

She softened a bit, "No, Tara, Be who you are, but just care more about people than knowledge. Knowledge isn't everything you know."

Tara sniffed, "I don't have to deal with this right now," she promptly put her pillow over her head and plugged her ears.

*******************************************

"Oh, I wish I was in Dixie away in my lovely bed away…" Beck sang heartily behind Xander, too tired and bored to care. Suddenly, he tripped on a log that was hidden in the fallen leaved on the ground. As he reached out to catch himself on the hedge wall, he grabbed a thorn, which sank deep into his hand. He screamed in pain.

Alexander dropped beside him, grabbing his bleeding hand; he pulled the thorn out with his other hand. Beck's face ashened, "Beck! Beck! Are you okay? Can you walk?" No response from Beck as he lay limp on the ground, his eyes already closed. Alexander quickly wound his handkerchief, spreading his cloak out on the ground, he carefully rolled Beck over onto it. Taking Beck's cloak off was no easy task, but he finally managed to roll his limp friend around enough to wiggle it out from under him.

Xander tied Beck's cloak to his and took off his and Beck's belts. Carefully ripping slits in Beck's cloak with the thorn. He slipped the buckle of his Belt through the slit he had cut in the cloak and Beck's belt's other end buckling them together. He then threaded the two remaining belt ends into his belt loops and buckled them.

Reaching into his pocket, he pulled out his dorm straw. It immediately sprang to life and pointed in the direction to go. Alexander to a step straining with the extra weight. He took another one. "Jiminy," He muttered to himself, "Once he's better, I am going to lock him away to starve for a while."

Alexander thought that previous thought about eight thousand times by the time he saw the exit of the maze. He started yelling for help. He saw Carethemost and Skane running toward him as he collapsed in the dust exhausted. His vision blurred, and the lamp light faded as he fell into blissful sleep.

# Chapter 12
# Clues

Alexander awoke to birds chirping and a sweet melody. An older lady dressed as a nurse was humming to herself as she watered flowers on the window sill. The sun rose brightly through the windows of the hospital room.

Glancing around, he saw Beck. And there was Mrs Good sleeping in bed as well.

"Oh, you're awake! How do you feel, young man?" The nurse lady asked him cheerfully.

"I'm fine. How's Beck?" He glanced over at Beck, who still looked rather pale.

The nurse looked at him a bit sadly, "The poison from the thorn paralyzed him; he is in a coma."

Alexander fought off tears, "What about Mrs Good?" He asked.

The nurse glanced around and then leaned down close, "If you ask me, I believe she was poisoned by the thorn, too."

BOOM! The doors to the hospital swung open, and Carethemost and Amatus strolled in. Seeing Alexander alive and well, Amatus smiled, "Good to see you are awake, lad. How's the other one?" Amatus looked somber as he turned to Carethemost, "I want those shrub thorns burnt immediately. Today. We can't have any other students being harmed."

Carethemost nodded, "I agree. I will assemble a burning squad and see to it personally." He turned on his heel and strolled out of the doors.

Amatus turned to the nurse, "Is it the same poison, Nancy?"

"I am not certain," She replied, shaking her head slightly, "But whatever poisoned Mrs Good is very similar if not the same to Beck's poisonous thorn.

Amatus looked at her thoughtfully, glancing between Beck and Mrs. Good, lying there so still, "I notified the teachers to be on the lookout for an unknown person, bit I doubt we will find anything. There are close to 2,000 rooms on the school grounds alone." He shook his head as he walked to Alexander's side. "I fear the Soul Snatcher knows you are here. Be wary and NEVER go outside alone. Okay?"

Alexander nodded somberly, "Yes, Sir."

***************************

Alexander looked at Beck's still-empty lower bunk. It had been weeks since the maze incident. They had played Begotten again, with Henry successfully winning the Earth dorm a second key. The scores were now Grey Dorm one key, Yellow Dorm two, Green Dorm two, Blue Dorm one, and Red Dorm zero. There was one more game yet this year, and all the teams were planning their winning strategies.

Everyone had forgiven him for losing the one game since they heard how he had drug Beck from the maze. But he did not feel very heroic. He and Lucy ate together, but they didn't say much. He tried to go to the pigeon farm, but the headmaster wouldn't let him go. Dr. Skane was as good and kind as ever, which made him doubt himself about Dr. Skane being the poisoner.

Alexander flopped back in his bed. Confused and bothered, he had a nagging feeling that the mystery still wasn't over.

"Snake! Snake!" Jeffrey, a younger boy from his dorm, came running in headed for Henry's room. "Henry, Come quick! There's a snake in the yard.".

Alexander just got down from his bunk and followed the other students as they all ran for the edge of the yard, close to the forest. There, coiled up in the grass, was a five-foot chicken snake. Its tongue darted in and out of its mouth. Henry began to approach it slowly with a stick clutched in his hand.

"Halt Boy!" A round little woman bustled up to the growing crowd of students, all trying to crowd close enough to take a good look at what was happening but staying far enough away, they didn't have to worry too much about getting struck by the nasty reptile.

Xander didn't recognize the woman from anywhere on campus. Her hair framed her face in frizzy curls, and her mouth looked too small to fit with her round face. Clenched tightly in her hand was a 3-foot bat the children used for ball games when they weren't playing Begotten.

The little woman quickly came around behind the snake and whopped it solidly on the head. "There see. You should always approach a snake from the rear. I've been trying to catch this little devil for some time now. He's been eating all my pigeons."

The students all stared in awe at her. She was apparently new and exciting. Exceptionally different from their strict teachers.

The woman looked around at all the students, whose eyes were still glued to her and the bat in her hand. She wrinkled her brow and said, "Well, stop staring at me. It's rude. Here, boy, wack it a few more times." She handed the bat to Xander, who cautiously reached out and hit the snake on the head. Rapidly, he stepped back to the edge, away from it.

The woman grinned and said, "Okay, I'll take the snake and throw it in the woods. Goodbye!" She grabbed the snake and strolled off as relaxed as she could.

"Wow, she's crazy!"

"You see how she just whacked it?"

"And it didn't even affect her.".

The children all spoke excitedly. Xander stood watching her walk away with a touch of admiration, along with the other students.

Suddenly, he remembered that he still held her bat. He started running after her as she disappeared into the forest.

Alexander finally reached the edge of the woods. He glanced around for any sign of where she had gone. But she had disappeared among the thick underbrush. Alexander sighed and turned slowly. He walked back toward the academy. He systematically walked into the classroom and sat down at his desk, still thinking about the strange woman.

"Oooo, pouty boy. You gonna cry?" Marstin heckled him, trying to goad him into anger. But Alexander stared into space. His mind was completely removed from this world; he was oblivious to the nagging boy.

Dr. Skane walked into the classroom. He stared at Marstin. Marstin looked down quickly and tried to pretend he wasn't doing anything. His ear still tingled from his last encounter with Alexander and Dr. Skane. He hurriedly retreated to his desk, and the class got ready to pull their workbooks out and begin studying.

Before anyone could start reading, Dr. Skane interrupted, "One second, students." They all looked up, surprised. "I asked Headmaster Carethemost if we could have a field trip to give us some fresh air away from the school and classes. So if you will, Please follow me."

Excited gasps came from all the students as they happily put away their books and followed Dr. Skane out the main doors of the academy. He led them, right? Winding his way through the trees that lined the turnaround that led to the academy. He continued on from here to his right. The burned ashes of where the maze used to be could be seen in the distance. Dr. Skane continued walking.

"Where are we going, Alexander?" Lucy asked as she came up beside Xander.

"I don't know." Alexander shrugged and kept walking.

Dr. Skane stopped. Bending down, he wrote on the ground. Out from the grass rose a transparent doorway decorated with gold and precious jewels such as rubies and emeralds. On either side of the doorway was a large turntable with a circular handle.

Dr. Skane turned toward the class and asked, "Where would you like to go hiking?"

Puzzled, no one replied. They just stood there, staring at him.

Dr. Skane smiled and said, "Very well, I'll pick." He turned the handle. Immediately, a picture appeared in the doorway. An island with moss-covered rocks and valleys of daisies. Trees spread their leaf-covered branches, providing shade. Well-warned trails showed a testament to other student hikers before them.

"Come on," students, Dr. Skane led the way. Stepping through the doorway and disappearing. The students were astounded. Jonathan looked behind the doorway, but nothing was there except fields of green grass.

Alexander walked toward the door. Taking a deep breath, he stepped through. A light wind rustled his dark hair as he gazed at the scenery of winding hiking trails leading upward to what looked like a lookout tower.

Dr. Skane stood there, smiling at him. "Beautiful, isn't it?"

Alexander turned and looked back at the doorway full of peering faces as the other students attempted to see them. "It's amazing, truly! It's like a one-way mirror to..." Alexander looked at his teacher and asked, "Where all does it go?"

Skane continued smiling as he watched him. "To more places than I can tell you. That doorway is a portal to wherever you want to go. For instance, I wanted to go hiking, so I spun the handle, and it brought me to a lovely hiking spot."

Alexander watched as the other student slowly started cautiously walking through the portal. Once everyone was through, Dr. Skane led the way up the trail, with Tara right on his heels. Lucy and Alexander brought up the rear.

**Clues**

"Have you talked to Tara lately?" Xander looked at Lucy.

Lucy shook her head and frowned. "She's stuck up and won't talk to me right now. And she's forever hurrying around, like in a trance of sorts. Like she's not sure where to go next."

Xander shrugged and squinted in the sun to where Tara was headed up the hill right behind Dr. Skane. "We should just let bygones be bygones, I guess. I'm sure if Beck recovers, he will love to hold that over her head till death do them part." They both burst out laughing at the thought. Then Xander sobbed a bit. "But as for me, I don't hold anything against her."

Lucy thought for a moment: "Maybe we should give her a gift for her birthday next week."

Xander grinned, "Agreed! That's a really good idea. But what would she want?"

Lucy sighed. "Probably some book.".

The children enjoyed the sunshine and chirping birds. The boys found sticks and proceeded to have epic duels with one another. The girls picked flowers and made head crowns and necklaces. A crystal-clear brook ran through the trail, and they waded and splashed each other. Others practiced skipping stones downstream after Dr. Skane showed them how to hold and throw the rocks.

A game of hide and seek ensued, with students running and diving behind trees, trying to beat the tagger back to base. Once everyone was tired from both running and giggling, They flopped down on the cool grass in the shade. The joys of being young and free were evident.

Dr. Skane got up from where he had been leaning against a tree. He called to his students, "Okay, boys and girls. It's time to go back to the academy." Groans and protests echoed throughout the group following his words, but everyone got up and started gathering the different treasures they had collected and headed toward the portal that would take them back to AGE.

Alexander followed the group. Suddenly, he stopped, noticing a drawing on the ground. Upon taking a closer look, he realized it was his name drawn in the dirt with a line through it.

As he stood there looking at the drawing, Lucy called his name. He ignored her and stepped closer, almost directly on top of the drawing. That's when the ground gave way. He yelled and tried to grab the edge of the hole to drag himself up on the trail. His fingers slipped through the silty dirt.

Lucy screamed his name and dove. Grabbing his hand, he yelled for Dr. Skane, who came running over. When he saw what was happening, Xander was barely holding on to the edge, while Lucy looked like she was about to fall into the hole right after him. He yelled for Marstin, "Come, Marstin, grab her other hand."

Marstin stood there, rooted for a moment. Unwilling to save his Nemesis but knowing the consequences of using the dark work of defiance, he rushed forward and helped Dr. Skane pull Alex from the hole.

"Thank you!" Dr. Skane panted, patting Marstin on the shoulder. Then, turning to a still very frightened Xander, he spoke, "Well, Alexander, I would say it's safe to say fate does not like you." He held a stone above the hole and then, releasing it, allowed it to drop. Twenty seconds later, he heard the plunk as the stone hit the water.

Dr. Skane stood and brushed his pants off, giving Alexander a hand. He looked toward the group and said, "Okay, everyone. Back to school. Drew led the way. I will follow behind and keep an eye out for anything else that would want to harm anyone."

Skane walked behind the row of students as they meandered their way up the hill toward the portal. He glanced behind himself, frequently assuring their safety, as he did not see anything that could be a threat. They stepped through the portal one at a time. All were very relieved to be back at AGE, even after the fun they had.

# Chapter 13
# The Final Game

"All right, everybody! Listen up!" Henry stood at the front of the oldest boys' room. He had gathered the boys and girls together before the last game of the year. "We're tied with the gray team. Sadly, Beck is still unable to play, but I know we can win with teamwork and determination. Who's with me?"

The students cheered and yelled together, all enthusiastically agreeing with their captain. Alexander smiled and slapped Beck on the shoulder. It had been a very happy day when Nurse Nancy found Xander, telling him Beck was awake and well. Howbeit is sore and weak from such a long hospital stay.

"You've got this, Alexander. Just watch out for Marstin. He'll focus on you and eliminate you first." Beck was chirpier than ever, but he didn't have the strength to run for long periods of time. Thus, he was not playing in the final game.

Xander nodded absentmindedly. "I'll watch him." He promised, staring off gloomily into space.

Beck wrinkled his brow. "What's wrong with you?"

"I don't know. I just have a feeling I've missed something, and I can't figure out what it is. And I still feel like I'm being watched.".

Beck slapped Xander on the back. "Just don't think about it. Maybe it will go away."

Alex shrugged. Maybe Beck was right. Maybe he was just being paranoid. Maybe nobody was out to get him. Maybe....

**********************************

Excitement was raging throughout the dorms as each team got into their uniforms. The boys pretended to jump and dodge with the precious key, and the girls relaxed. They enjoyed singing, so they didn't really care. Especially the younger ones.

Lucy and Tara had finally made some sort of peace. Although Tara was still reserved and quiet, Beck rattled endlessly in Alexander's ear, telling him how to dodge and swerve properly. Even the teachers were excited and preening themselves, for the council had decided to come watch along with the royal families.

Chairs covered in fur had been set out for the coming guests. Each family was nearest to their children's team. Banners had been made to represent each team.

A red banner with flames spreading across its entirety. The green banner displayed the Earth; mighty waves crashing decorated the blue banner; and the yellow banner represented air, which is pretty hard to represent due to its translucency. So, the banner was plain yellow. And lastly, the gray banner representing Space displayed that of a shooting star through Space.

The banners were attached to eight-foot flag poles at each base. Easily being able to be moved when the teams switched places.

The parents started arriving by fancy cars, puttering smoke and clanging with noise. If the engine stopped, the driver would get out and manually spin the crank at the front to get it started again. Some families rode in long, 12-wheel carriages pulled by magnificent steeds. Previous students to the academy had been hired as lackeys and car parkers.

The holly lady who had killed the snake previously also came to the game. Attending to the horses. Taking them across the way to her farm to water and care for them during the game.

The teachers greeted all the parents as they came and led them to their appointed seats. Head Bishop Amatus appeared, accompanied by Deacon Jhos and Head Minister Segundo. They shook hands with teachers and parents, as well as former students. The Head Bishop, Minister, Deacon, and Headmaster chairs were pyramided from smaller to bigger. The biggest chair was in the center, with the smaller ones on either side.

Amatus sat in the center chair, enjoying the hustle and bustle of the excited viewers and players. Musicians softly played in the background.

The teams filed out amidst much applause and whistling from the crowd. Each team walked to their elected bases. When the teams were all there and ready, Maximus took the raised platform. Holding an opened gourd against his lips, "WELCOME TO THE FIFTH AND FINAL GAME OF THE YEAR!" Clapping and yelling ensued as he continued, "Two teams have the chance to win a special trip to the garden. The other teams have only to capture the key, and the prize will be held off until next year. Good luck to everyone." And so, he blew the starting horn.

The teams launched at each other. Some succeeded in making it to the center base. Others were eliminated but retrieved back into the game by their revengeful teammates. Sweat and dust marked the player's faces.

The gray team was front and center. Guarding the key like ravenous wolves. They huddled around those who managed to grab the key but needed to escape back to their base from the center. Suddenly, a boy about Alexander's age burst out from the center. Key in hand, intent on scoring a point for Red.

Marstin saw him running out of the corner of his eye and ran towards him. Without attempting to be gentle, he pushed the boy to the ground and, with a "ha," grabbed the key and returned it to its stand.

Multiple attempts were made, but none were more than ten feet away from the center before being eliminated. The horn sounded, and the teams switched. The green team is taking the center. Once again, the horn sounded, and the teams launched once again into a flurry.

Alexander eliminated the layer and then another boy grabbed the key and took off. Alexander launched himself into the air and caught his foot. The boy grunted as he hit the ground, and the air whooshed out of his lungs. He grinned at Alex and said, "Nice tag; I almost had it." Xander grinned back and returned the key once again to the center.

On and on it went. The green team's time in the center was no more than 15 minutes, but it felt like an eternity. Their time was finally up, and the Yellow team took the center.

The key changed hands. An older boy handed it off to a fellow teammate. She almost made it only five feet from the safety of her base. Henry caught her as he ran for the green base. Ivan, from the Yellow team, tagged him and brought the key back to the center.

With two minutes left on the massive clock that was on the stand, Mr. Maximus was still standing. Henry motioned for Alexander after Ivan was eliminated. "Remember what I told you when all else fails?" Alexander grinned as he remembered. He had practiced it over and over in his head at night. They both fell into step. Henry dodged a player and succeeded in getting to the center.

Alexander ran back and forth to avoid defenders and other attackers. The prophecy of Alexander had gotten around, and every player was intent on proving they were better than the 'prophecy boy,' and everyone wanted a chance to say they eliminated him in at least a game.

What Henry wanted was for Alexander to get close. Then run back to base. Seemingly to develop a pattern. Suddenly, Henry saw his chance as the boy guarding him turned his head as Xander fell dramatically. As planned, Henry snatched the key and booked it for their base. His long legs carried him rapidly across the field. Other players yelled in hopelessness as Henry crossed into the safety of their base.

Confetti shot into the air as people shouted. My teammates yelled and jumped around, celebrating. The field was packed with families celebrating as well as congratulating and hugging their children. Henry explained his scheme to his teammates, explaining that it was Xander's victory as much as his. They lifted both Henry and Xander into the air and transported them into the Great Hall in great spirits.

# Chapter 14
# Ensnared

The Grand Hall was alive with noise and loud celebrations. The green banner was brought inside and placed in the center of the room. The circle table surrounding it. A large table at the head of the circle was folded out of the floor for the council members, families, and teachers.

The table was laden with meats, cheeses, lemonades, and countless sweets and treats. Alexander and Henry were placed where the teachers originally sat; Beck, Lucy, and Tara lined up beside Xander while Henry's friends gathered around him.

Marstin sat morosely on the farthest end possible with? And?. Both were trying to cheer him up but to no avail.

The Headmaster stood up, hushing the flamboyant students, "Our Head Bishop would like to say a few words and bless our meal. And before he does, I have a few words." He smiled and looked at the overjoyed winners. "To the winners, well done. You succeeded. To our less fortunate: Don't despair. You all did your very best, and that's what matters. You can make another attempt next year. Thank you!" And with that, he took his seat.

Amatus rose to his feet, raising his hands, and blessed the meal, giving thanks. Afterward, he stayed standing and addressed the crowd, "Well, I enjoyed the activities of this evening very much. You students are the world of tomorrow—the leaders, teachers, and faithful followers of the light. Well done to all of you."

The feast began with ripples of laughter, and excessive chatter echoed throughout. Alexander was about sick and tired of slaps on the back, and congratulations were echoing in his ears. He and Beck talked about the end of the term and what they would do this winter. They were released from the academy for three months in the winter.

## Ensnared

Beck was going to a skiing resort. Lucy was vacationing on a small island on the coast, and Tara was off in LaLa Land, not paying attention to what they were discussing. Therefore, she did not mention what she would be doing or where she would be going. Alexander didn't have plans but knew his mama would most likely put him to work doing random chores.

Students dispersed into groups. Enjoying games of 20 Square and Egg Beater. The older ones enamored them with tall tales and stories. The teachers brought the families up to speed on life at the academy, and the council mingled attentively with everyone.

"Let's go play a round of 20 squares." Beck pulled Alexander to the traced-out squares in the corner. Twenty students stood, each in their own square, and tried to bounce the ball into each other's squares. You could be eliminated. If the ball landed in your square or you tried to hit another player's square and failed, If you hit a ball and it hit a line or landed outside someone's square, you were eliminated. If eliminated, you had to go to the back of the assembly line of children behind the first square.

The goal was to become a server, or even better, a two-time server, which meant you eliminated server 1, moved into his spot, and then eliminated server 2, claiming the second server spot, which is a very hard spot to hold because if you are hit with a ball, you are eliminated.

Lucy and Beck started first and were able to move up rapidly to the higher squares. Alexander failed to make it past square three. He repeated this cycle for quite a while. One square, two square, three square, out!! It seemed he was always back in the back of the line. Eventually, he got bored and left the game to wander the halls and think.

He wandered back and forth, looking at the timeline on the wall. Reading the information board for known news from families and former students. One family was on an outreach. Another was selling the newest and best hand tools and carriage parts.

After a while, he walked towards the left side dorms. He strolled around the flower-covered turnabout as he thought to himself that he had decided to go back and enjoy the festivities. So what if it was amazingly loud? It was his last night here at the academy for this year, and he was going to enjoy it as best he could.

As he turned back towards the blazing Grand Hall, he noticed a dim red light shining from a shuttered dorm window. He only noticed it as one of the shutters appeared to be broken off and allowed an inch of light to shine through. Approaching it, he peeked inside. The room walls were bare. On the floor was a circle. Strew about were straw feathers, and sticks weaved together. The light that was shimmering out was a heated lamp of sorts, pointing directly at the huge nest.

Alexander jumped back. The realization dawned: everything (almost everything) fell into place. He rushed for the grand hall. He burst through the double doors and ran to Beck, who had just gotten eliminated.

"Beck! Beck!" Alexander grabbed Beck's arm, gasping for air. "Where's Lucy and Tarah?" He managed to gasp.

Beck turned and looked at him incredulously. "There you are. Where did you go?"

Xander shook his head. "No time to explain. Where are the girls?"

Beck looked around and said, "Umm, well, Lucy was right there getting a drink a second ago, and Tara?" He scanned the crowd, shrugging.

Xander was annoyed at Beck's relaxed response. He bolted toward Lucy. "Where's Tara?" Lucy looked at him, startled, her mouth full of lemonade. She turned and let her finger point randomly. Not finding Tara, she swallowed and answered.

"I don't really know. She was just here.".

Xander looked around, trying to find any of the teachers. Not seeing any of them, he muttered to himself and ran for the door.

**Ensnared**

Beck drank in hand and watched Xander run for the door; Lucy grabbed his hand, sending Beck's drink flying, liquid spilling on his shirt. "Let's go. He seems like something is urgent."

"Oh, come on, Lucy! My favorite shirt." Beck whined as he was drug unceremoniously to the exit.

Lucy barely glanced back at him but gave a hurried, "Sorry. But we gotta follow Xander."

They came around the corner to the dorm entrance to meet Xander, who had dashed to his dorm and returned with the bat he got from Judy, the jolly farmer lady.

"What exactly are you doing?" Huffed, Beck glared at Xander for his lack of explanation.

"We gotta find Tarah," Xander glanced around. A lantern light flashed from the edge of the Swamp of Hatred. He sprinted for it, yelling over his shoulder, "It's him!"

Lucy and Beck ran after their fleeing friend, completely and utterly thinking Xander was losing his mind. Him Who?

✶✶✶✶✶✶✶✶✶✶✶✶✶✶✶✶✶✶✶

Marstin watched as the three students ran out of the Grand Hall door. He motioned for? And?. They reached the outdoors just in time to catch a glimpse of the runaways heading across the yard under the ever-darkening sky.

✶✶✶✶✶✶✶✶✶✶✶✶✶✶✶✶✶✶✶✶

The lantern light led off through the swamp. Beck balked at the edge and said, "No, Xander, there are alligators in there." He shook his head, slowly backing away from the edge.

93

Xander reached back and grabbed his shirt, pulling him forward. "You gotta trust me, Beck; I think Tara is in danger."

The mud sucked at their shoes as they maneuvered through the eight-foot reeds and cattails. Cypress Knees rose up from the mud and water, threatening to trip them. Xander led the way, holding his wooden bat in front of him like a sword. He stopped listening briefly. Not a sound could be heard. No frogs, no birds, not even a mosquito buzzing. It was eerily silent. He felt that familiar lump forming in the pit of his stomach. He swallowed, and they pushed on.

The three pressed on, checking for the lantern by climbing a rare tree they came across. Seeing the lantern in the distance, they pressed on.

Suddenly, they entered a clearing fifteen feet in diameter. Directly across from them stood Tara, her back turned away from them, facing a man.

"Tara!" Xander called out to her. Tara turned slowly to look at him as the man looked up.

"Well, my trap has succeeded after all."  He grinned horribly at Xander.

"Let her go," Xander demanded

The man smiled again. "Oh, her? Immediately. You're the one I wanted all along. She was just a pawn." He pushed Tara toward them, causing her to stumble and fall. Lucy and Beck rushed over to her. The man watched them reach her and said, "It took me months to hypnotize her. It's a lot harder than you would imagine."

"So that's where she was the day we broke into your room!" Beck glared at Dr. Skane.

Skane laughed evilly. "Smart boy. I started out slow. When she would study by the windows, I would lay outside and look deep into her eyes. Subconsciously, she gave her will to me slowly but surely."

Alexander stepped forward, pointing his stick toward Skane. "So it was you that poisoned Mrs. Good?" He accused, glaring.

"Right again, ole chap. I simply placed a thorn from the maze on her desk chair and waited. Then, when she was poisoned, I hypnotized her as well, so she can never recover without my saying so." He grinned, enjoying their horror. "Then I made sure you and Beck had to get in trouble and go through the maze leading to the burning of it, which erased all evidence of what had poisoned dear Mrs. Good." He clapped sadistically. "I do give you a hand, Alexander, for getting into my room. Luckily, I had put up my bed already."

Alexander remembered something. Reaching his hand into his pocket, he pulled out a feather. Dr. Skanes eyes slit in anger. Xander grinned. "You packed up all but this lonely pigeon feather, which I found on your floor. It confused me till I saw your nest tonight!" Alexander tossed the feather onto the ground.

Skane grimaced as his body shook. His hair and ears disappeared. A forked tongue moved rapidly in and out of his mouth. Scaled appeared on his body, and the children watched in shocked horror as he transformed into a thirty-foot serpent.

"RUNNNNNN!" Xander yelled. Lucy and Beck grabbed Tara and ran. Beck opened his hand, and his straw sprang to life, pointing in the direction of safety.

Xander dodged behind a tree as Skane, the snake, struck at him. As the snake recoiled for another strike, Xander raced after the others. He tripped on a cypress tree. He fell just as Skane struck again. Their bodies collided.

"Come now, Alexander. The Soul Snatcher would make you into a great man." Xander kicked and wiggled free. The snake slithered around into a coil. "He told me to keep you alive and persuade you to join us in the final rebellion. Come with Usssssssss!" Skane hissed as he looked deep into Alexander's eyes, moving ever closer by the second.

Alexander felt whoozy. His will to resist was slipping away. A rock hit Skane. He whirled, hissing toward Lucy and Beck, who stood ready, armed with more rocks. Beck stuck his thumbs in his ears and wiggled his fingers, trying to taunt the beast. Skane shrieked and rushed at him. Beck yelled, "Yikes, bad idea, my bad. Run, Lucy!"

Lucy rolled her eyes as she turned and ran. "Duh, genius, what else am I going to do? Challenge the thirty-foot killer snake into a game of rock, paper, scissors."

Xander shook his head, the trance broken on him. He ran toward Skane, yelling.

Beck and Lucy grabbed Tara from where they had left her. She helped as best as she could, but after months of being controlled, she was left feeling weak and helpless. As they were running, Beck lost his footing on a loose limb, causing the three of them to fall. Lucy saw the lights of the academy up ahead as she fell.

Skane was quickly upon them: "Little wretched, prepare for your doom."

WHAMMMMMMMM

Skane recoiled and shook. Alexander had run up his back and clobbered him on the head with his bat. Skane twisted, screeching and throwing Alex off balance. He plummeted his back into the swamp, striking his head on a stump. Lucy screamed in terror.

Skane wiggled in the yard, dying. He fell onto the grass, his yellow eyes staring into nothing. With his dying hiss, he cursed Alexander, and then everything was silent.

Beck and Lucy scrambled for Alexander. Tara, released completely from the Skanes trance, followed them on her own.

Lights began to appear as teachers rushed toward the swamps. Amatus had heard Lucy's scream, and quieting the students, he, Carethemost, and Segundo had rushed outside. Mr. Shy held the students in the grand hall, awaiting to hear the outcome of what had caused the scream.

## Ensnared

Nurse Nancy almost gave up on the ghost when Mrs. Good bolted upright and started screaming. Mrs. Good was released like Tara the moment Skane died.

The three men made their way toward the swamp lanterns held high. Amatus spotted the giant serpent first.

"There! A snake, gentlemen!" He pointed a finger. As they slowly approached. Marstin and his friends stepped out of the darkness into the lantern light Segundo held.

Marstin held Alexander's bat; it had been knocked from his hand when he fell. "I saved their lives!" Marstin boasted, slapping the bat resoundingly against his opposite hand.

"Who's? Boy, tell me!" Carethemost grabbed him and shook him.

Marstin's eyes widened. He was expecting immediate praise, not questioning. He began his story by watching Lucy, Beck, and Alexander go into the swamp. Then he told them how the snake was about to eat them, and he knocked the snake on the head, killing it.

The Head Bishop looked at Marstin's companions and asked, "Is this story true?" Both boys looked at each other and nodded viciously.

"Yes, Sir. Every word is true."

Segundo smiled and said, "You have done well. Very well indeed!"

Amatus frowned as if not quite believing the story but did not comment. He motioned to? "Go get Nurse Nancy; we need to get the others away from the swamp as fast as possible." The three men ran for the swamp.

# Epilogue

Alexander awoke with the sun streaming through the window of his dorm. He lifted his hand to his pounding head and felt a bandage. He slowly sat up and swung his feet over the side of the bed. Taking a moment as the world spun around him. He haltingly pulled on his school clothes. As he was bent over, tying his shoes, Beck burst in.

"Xander! You're alive! And awake!" Alexander grimaced as he sat up straight. His head was pounding even harder at Beck's joyous outburst.

"Yep, I'm alive. What happened?"

"You hit your head really hard when Skane threw you. Mr. Carethemost, Amatus, and Segundo found us and took you to the infirmary. Nurse Nancy wrapped your head, and then we brought you here."

Xander grimaced again as Beck was still shouting in excitement. "What happened to Skane?"

"Well, he turned back into a man after three days.".

Xander's eyes widened. "Three days?"

Beck nodded. "Yup, three whole days. You've been unconscious for three days."

Xander shook his head in disbelief. "Did you tell the headmaster what happened?"

Beck's eyes fell, then filled with anger. "We tried. All of us went to Carethemost and told him what happened. But Marstin had the bat with blood on it, so it was three against three. So he took us all to Amatus."

Alexander glared. Jumping in, he said, "First, tell me what Marstin said.".

Beck reiterated the tall tale, which had grown so big and out of this world that hardly any of the details were even believable. But most everyone believed it. "Marstin now says he knew all along Skane was going to try to kill, which isn't exactly true because Skane wanted to try to sway you first. But anyway, Marstin described it as if we were cowards behind him, and he fought off Skane singlehandedly, and Skane, as a last resort, tried to kill you by using his tail to fling you." Beck stopped for a breath and stood there, shaking with anger, as he was reminded once again of Marstin's jeering, triumphant face.

Xander mulled it all over, bewildered. He never thought all of this would occur. He wasn't upset as much as he was disappointed in human nature. Finally, he looked at Beck and said, "What did Amatus say?"

"He said he would wait until you woke up and heard your story before casting judgment."

Xander nodded. "How's Tara and Lucy?"

Beck laughed. Xander grinned. "Fine, let's go see them.".

The boys walked outside. Henry was the first to greet them. "Well, well, look who's up and kicking. Glad to see you better." He clasped Xander on the back in passing.

Xander thanked him and moved on. A few more students commented that they were glad to see he was alive before the boys finally spotted Lucy.

"Lucy," Xander called out. Lucy spun around and ran toward them with a huge grin on her face. She hugged Xander tight.

"Thank goodness you're better. Did Beck tell you what happened?"

Xander nodded as he hugged her back. "Oh well. So be it. How's Tara?" Lucy rolled her eyes and pointed to where Tarah was arguing with an older student about the Cornelius Effect.

Alexander laughed. "Back to normal then, eh?" They all stood grinning at Tarah, who noticed them at length. She stopped her argument, agreeing to finish it when they both had more time. They split ways, and Tarah walked over.

"About time you woke up," she snapped.

Alexander grinned and said, "Good to see you too." The children began rehashing the events of that terrifying night. As they were talking, Alexander heard his name being called. Turning, he saw Headmaster Carethemost headed toward them. "Hey, Carethemost wants us. Let's go!" The children all turned and walked toward the headmaster, who waited for them at the entrance of the academy.

As they neared him, he spoke, "Amatus would like to see you four. He is waiting in his office. Alexander, you know the way. Please lead on. Be back in time for lunch." So he said he held the door for them. Closing it firmly behind them, he disappeared into the Grand Hall.

The children arrived at the twelve-door hall. Alexander found the correct door, and they entered quickly and quietly.

Mr. Amatus sat in his chair by the fire. He smiled at them as they entered. "Good Morning!" He quipped cheerfully.

"Good morning." The children echoed back as they settled into the plush leather seats.

"I'm so glad to see you are all well. Especially you, Alexander. We were getting worried when you didn't wake up right away. Also, I am glad to see that you, Tarah, are back to your full cognitive ability." He turned, focusing on Beck and Lucy for a moment. "To you two, I would like to say thank you for being true to Alexander and Tarah. That kind of faithfulness is hard to find."

Amatus paused for a moment, his elbows resting on his desk and his chin resting on his clasped hands. "Now I know the dispute that is currently circling the school, so please, Alexander, if you would, please tell me your side of the story."

Alexander started quietly at first, but at length, as he got excited, he started talking full steam. He told of the bedroom, the swamps, and the snake/Dr. Skane. He also detailed the events of the year leading up to Skane's demise. Then he trailed off, running out of words. He sat back down in his seat. He hadn't realized he had stood up in the middle of his excitement.

Amatus sat back in his chair, thoughtful for a moment. The only sound in the room was the giant clock ticking in the corner. After a moment, Amatus spoke: "Do you have any questions?" Alexander nodded. Amatus motioned for him to speak.

"Why didn't Beck and I see the bed when we opened the door the first time?"

Amatus replied, "Dr. Skane was very crafty and smart. It's a wonder he didn't see that one feather left behind, and it is even more surprising that he had his bed folded into the ceiling without any of us even knowing that his room could do that." Amatus looked worried. "Which means that when we built these buildings, someone had planned for that exact purpose."

Alexander looked alarmed. "Does that mean that someone planned for me to arrive twenty years in advance?"

Amatus mulled Xander's question over for a moment. "That is possible. There were many people working here. It could have been anyone. I had hoped that after this incident, it would be the end, but I wouldn't let my guard down."

At length, the children said their goodbyes. Amatus assured them that he believed their story and that the truth would come out eventually. He did promise to inform the council and the teacher of the truth, as well as the parents.

Happily, Alexander, Beck, Tarah, and Lucy rode the elevator back to AGE.

Amatus, however, stared long into the fire, considering. He arose and walked to his desk. Opening his bottom drawer, he reached deep into it and opened the trap door that concealed the fake bottom. He drew forth a leather-bound book. Opening it, he ran his eyes over the page. The names of people who were present at the building of the academy.

He sighed, rubbing his hands through his hair. The names on the paper were the names of his eleven council members.

*To be continued.........*